靈媒的故事

成 寒◎編著

The Psychic

目　錄　CONTENTS　靈媒的故事

靈媒的故事
──有聲故事內文

聽力測驗

延伸閱讀

如何使用本書

《靈媒的故事》是一則發人深省的故事，
透過情境式的有聲書娓娓道來。

學習方法：
請參閱《英文，非學好不可》及
《早早開始，慢慢來》二書。

〔推薦序〕

輕鬆，但徹底的學英文

王 岫

成寒兩年前寫了《躺著學英文——聽力從零到滿分》，開始推廣以輕鬆的方式學習英文——邊玩邊學、躺著學、鬧著學，讓英文成為好玩的嗜好，跟跳舞一樣，一旦上了癮，就怎麼也戒不掉繼續學了。接著，她又陸續推出更能展現其理念的《躺著學英文 2 ——青春‧英語‧向前行》、《躺著學英文 3 ——打開英語的寬銀幕》等有聲書；《躺著學英文》三集在書市都引起讀者很熱烈的迴響，也是暢銷排行榜的「常」客和「長」客，這現象顯示的是一方面目前想學好英文，但不知從何著力的人的確很多，另一方面當然也是成寒的一些獨特、有趣的理念吸引大家。

當然，有時不免謗隨譽來。《躺著學英文》暢銷成名後，我看過一篇也是講如何學好英文的文章，似乎就意有所指地挖苦說：「學英文哪可以那麼容易，用躺著就可以學好？」作者可能沒把成寒的書全部讀完吧？——其實這誤會了成寒的本意：她要大家以輕鬆的方式來學英文，並不表示學好英文很輕鬆。

想一想，成寒在《躺著學英文——聽力從零到滿分》一書中說，她高中聯考英文只有個位數，到十七歲時英文還一團糟，擔心大學可能考不上，才激起她要學好英文的動機。在基礎不佳，信心全無的情況下，若不是摸索出一套有趣且輕鬆的學習方式，恐怕很難讓她能持久且快樂的學下去，不僅到國外讀書拿碩士，而且至今還樂在其中。

筆者再舉自己小女兒學英文的過程來印證。小女兒像現在的都會兒童一樣，小學三、四年級就開始到英文補習班學英文。那時的小學，學校還沒有英文課，所以補習班的英文課不必受到學校進度的影響，學習的壓力較小，加上外國老師大都比較活潑、開放，能和小朋友唱唱跳跳又互動頻繁；女兒在這種環境之下，培養了不怕英文，進而喜歡英文的基礎。但如果是像我小時候，到唸初中時才學英文，學校老師又以很嚴肅的方法教文法、閱讀，那英文就會像我一樣，一直在應付考試而老是學不好了。我相信成寒當年學不好英文可能也是這個原因。

由於對英文有興趣，也由於對國內國中教育環境有點不適應，小女兒在國中畢業時，自己透過學校申請到美國威州當一年國際交換學生。這一年當然就融入了成寒所說的完全的英語情境中，「聽」、「說」的能力大增，對英文的信心自然也大增。她回國後，能在電話中和她的寄宿家庭的爸、媽侃侃而談，令我羨慕；當然，我並不是提倡大家非得到美國去，在成寒《躺著學英文》系列書中，提到不少如何營造全面英語環境的方式，大家不妨參考。（編按：王青怡回來後寫了一本書《當小個兒遇上大塊頭》，記錄她當國際交換學生的經驗。）

女兒回國唸高中，不免又陷入聯考模式的讀英文方法中，好在她從成寒的書中獲得許多啟發，知道要另外多闢一些輕鬆而不枯燥的學習園地，所以她除了聽坊間英語雜誌外，也多聽一些有聲書（感謝成寒曾寄給她

《布魯克斯姊妹》（*The Brooks Sister*）、《美國短篇小說 1900-1950》（*American Short Stories 1900-1950*）和海明威《流動的饗宴》（*A Moveable Feast*）及英國詩人狄倫‧托瑪斯（Dylan Thomas）朗誦自己的詩……等錄音帶或光碟有聲書給她聽）；而且，她每周也常和我們去看電影或電視HBO影片，如同《躺著學英文 3 ──打開英語的寬銀幕》所說的，從寬銀幕中打開學習英語的新境界。因此，她的英文大致都能維持不錯的成績，在高二、高三也分別通過全民英檢的中級和中高級檢定。今年參加大學入學考試，英文考九十幾分，順利進入師範大學英語系就讀。

因此，以愉快的態度學英文，對英文的興趣才會持久，英文也才容易進步，這是《成寒英語有聲書》系列的主要宗旨。《成寒英語有聲書 1 ──綠野仙蹤》令人聽了就喜歡，許多讀者上她的留言版寫：綠野仙蹤真滴好好聽唷~^^真滴好好聽唷~^^。這次第二集推出的，是一齣情境式的英語故事──《靈媒的故事》，也是一部生動有趣的有聲書，故事本身發人深省，而錄製的手法讓人一聽就想繼續聽下去，在充滿知識性、故事性和趣味性的情境下學英語；這樣的英語有聲書，目前坊間真的不多見。這本書的字彙量只有1200左右，非常適合國中、高中學生來聽、讀，以輕鬆活潑的方式做到成寒所說的「繼續學習，徹底學習」。

（本文作者為國家圖書館參考組主任）

〔前言〕

從第六感生死戀到靈媒的故事

成　寒

　　看過《第六感生死戀》（*Ghost*）這部以人鬼戀為題材，闡述真愛永恆的浪漫愛情電影，有一段黛咪‧摩兒（Demi Moore）與派屈克‧史威茲（Patrick Swayze）兩人深情捏陶的情節，當四隻手重疊在陶土上，十指交握，我的心中只有你，你的心中只有我，那一幕令人感動得熱淚盈眶。然而，有一天不幸發生了，一方永遠離去，從此天人兩隔，他們唯一的溝通媒介就是女黑人琥碧戈柏（Whoopi Goldberg）飾演的靈媒。

　　「靈媒」（psychic）可說是一個特殊的民間信仰產物，顧名思義是與靈異溝通的媒介。他們以鬼魂附身，與前來問事的家屬對答，前往靈界，探訪與切身有關事物，尋求解決難題的方法。但靈媒也不一定是鬼魂附身，有的靈媒強調特異功能，所做的不僅如此而已，舉凡戀愛困境、家庭不合、生病、事業不順，人在徬徨無助時最需要所謂專家指點迷津，這時候，具「透視力」（clairvoyance）的靈媒適時扮演非常重要的角色，預卜未來、知道過去，與亡者通靈，還有夢的解析。

　　一般人總以好奇或敬畏或完全不相信的眼光，來看待靈媒不同於常人的特質。以我個人觀點而言，實在不太相信靈媒這樣的事，因為在現實生活中，無人去過天堂或地獄，也無人真正看過鬼魂——真的有嗎？大部分人只是聽說，或看過媒體報導，而無實際經歷可資佐證。

　　坊間相傳不少經由靈媒協助，將一些醫學上無法醫治與科學上無法解釋，不可莫名的一些事解決，如：嬰兒夜啼不眠，經靈媒收驚後得以安睡，或被害人託夢，指引兇手藏身之處，如《成寒英語有聲書2——靈媒的故事》一書中的情節。更聽說連自己都不太知道的事情，具「傳心術」（telepathy）的靈媒卻一語知人心。

　　靈媒是不是真的被附身？常人不得而知。也許他們有的是為了生計，唬弄顧客一番，假裝真的與陰陽界互通信息，裝神弄鬼騙人，恐怕連自己都不相信自己。但那就不叫靈媒，而是招搖撞騙的神棍。

　　但我相信靈媒有時也如心理輔導員或心靈導師，有疏導、安定人心與教化功能。只要不是裝神弄鬼，有其存在的功能，與不可思議的神妙之處。

　　兩則相關新聞報導：

2002/05/29

　　在華航空難中罹難的空服員徐惠婷，空難後，一直搜尋不著遺體。他們請來靈媒協尋，靈媒轉述惠婷的心意：「還有很多乘客在海裏，我要等他們都出來，才能走。」她的朋友既心疼又驕傲，因為她是那麼盡責，忠於職守，都默默為她祈禱。

　　　　　　＊　　　　　　　＊　　　　　　　＊

2003/11/12

　　歌手張雨生忌日當天，新聞台製作專題報導，請蒙著紅布條的女性靈媒到陰間尋找他，並接受記者「訪問」。訪談內容簡短，記者先問他對眾家好友翻唱他遺作的看法，他回答：「不是很滿意。」透過靈媒的口，

「張雨生」表示，「雨生歡禧城」紀念演唱會，他一定會到現場。

女歌手葉歡說：「我早就知道他一定會到！」而「東方快車」的主唱姚可傑則對張雨生表示歡迎，「這是他的場子，他怎麼可能不到？」張清芳甚至表示：「我跟他（指張雨生）早就約好了。」

＊　　　　　＊　　　　　＊

《成寒英語有聲書2──靈媒的故事》是一則發人深省的故事，原作者是保羅・維克多（Paul Victor），透過情境式的有聲書娓娓道來。一個命運坎坷的棄兒，一出生就被丟在公車上。為了生存他做小偷，後被關入牢裡。在獄中他認識一個哈佛名校畢業的老頭子，這人看出棄兒天資聰穎，於是教他讀書，說一口漂亮的英語，還有做靈媒的各種技巧：預卜未來、知道過去、與亡者通靈。

棄兒從小偷一變成為知名的靈媒，許多人來求問前途，連警方都來找他幫忙破案。然而年少輕狂，當年做錯了事，以為從此改頭換面就了結……最後的結局卻令人意想不到。

這本《成寒英語有聲書2——靈媒的故事》一如
《成寒英語有聲書1——綠野仙蹤》的特點,是「正常速
度」的英語,經由專業美語人士錄製而成的有聲書,逼
真的音效及生動的情節,讓人百聽不厭。如果您一直停
留在聽「慢速」英語的階段,建議您快快向前走吧!

以下是醫生作家莊裕安的十歲兒子聽了《成寒英語
有聲書1——綠野仙蹤》的心得:

開旭的第一個反應不是「難」,而是「快」。

其實現在的小孩講英文,已經慢到接近口吃,顯然英
語補習班或學校的老師因為教學,有不正常的慢。

這題材是他喜歡的,所以能靜下心來學習,好像拼很
難的樂高積木,小孩有出乎大人意料之外的耐心。

成寒在此感謝國家圖書館參考組主任王岫專文推
薦,好友紀元文博士及主編張敏敏校閱,以及林文理的
編輯。

　　＊請注意，在有聲故事內文中，為了讓讀者更容易閱讀，加了一些「他說」、「他嘆氣」諸如此類的補充文字。聽力測驗則完全一字一句對照有聲書的內容。

　　＊有關英文學習的問題，歡迎上〈成寒部落格〉：
http://www.wretch.cc/blog/chenhen

靈媒的故事

The Psychic

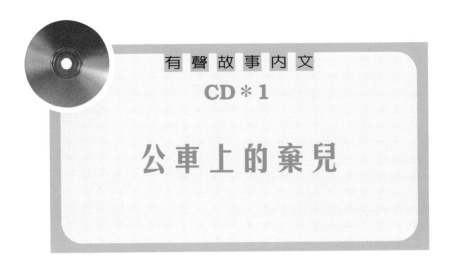

公 車 上 的 棄 兒

James Kenmore was a psychic.

People say: "A real psychic sees through time and space." It is a strange power. Not many people really have that power.

James Kenmore was a very successful psychic.

Rich people paid a lot of money for his help. They came to his office on Tremont Street. There they spoke to his receptionist, and the receptionist took them to his room. Brent had a big Cadillac car. He lived in a beautiful house. He was 50 years old.

▲肯摩爾是名氣響亮的靈媒。

He loved his wife and his two sons, and they loved him.

But Kenmore was not always successful. Oh, no. For the first 35 years of his life he was a failure. He *started* life a failure. He started without a father or a mother.

People found the baby James Kenmore on a Boston bus. Maybe his mother left him there? The bus **carried** people from **downtown** Boston to **Kenmore Square**, so they gave that name to the baby. He **grew up** in an **orphanage**—with 50 other children without mothers or fathers. The orphanage was 10 miles outside of Boston.

■ 內 文 提 示 :

1. psychic（*n.*）靈媒、通靈的人。

2. see through 洞察、透視、看穿。

3. A real psychic sees through time and space. 一個真正的靈媒能夠超越時間和空間，洞悉一切。

4. a lot of 許多的、大量的。

5. receptionist（*n.*）櫃檯人員、接待員。

6. Brent（*n.*）這裡是口誤，正確名字應該是 James。

7. Cadillac（*n.*）凱迪拉克轎車。

8. for the first 35 years of his life 他人生的前三十五年。

9. failure（*n.*）失敗、失敗者。

10. He started life a failure. 他一生下來就是個失敗者。

11. He started without a father or a mother. 他一生下來就沒有父母。

12. Boston（*n.*）波士頓：美國麻州首府。

13. carry（*v.*）載運。

14. downtown（*adj.*）市區的。

15. Kenmore Square 肯摩爾廣場：波士頓的區名。

16. grow up 長大。

17. orphanage（*n.*）孤兒院。

18. He grew up in an orphanage. 他在一家孤兒院長大。

19. The orphanage was 10 miles outside of Boston. 這家孤兒院位於波士頓郊外十英里。

命運多舛

At the age of 10, James Kenmore was in trouble with the police. He stole things from stores. He had to go to a home for bad children.

At the age of 15, he stole a car. For this he had to go to a boys' prison.

At 19, he was in trouble with the police again, and he went to a men's prison for the first time.

Why? Because he stole things from houses.

Kenmore was in prison for seven of the next ten years. He went there for two years, and then two

▲他誤入歧途，被關進少年監獄。

years again, and then three years. Between those
times in prison he always started work in a real job.
But he didn't like his work, and he was soon in trouble again.

The life of a **thief** was **interesting**, and his job
wasn't interesting. But he was not a smart thief. The

police always caught him. At the age of 30, they caught him again, and he went to prison for five years. In prison he met Stanley Tremaine.

Stanley Tremaine was a **con man**. He got money from people by **tricks**. He was a smart con man. The police never caught him, **up to** the age of 50. Then he tried a very big trick. They caught him, and he went to prison for seven years.

■ 內 文 提 示 ：

1. at the age of 10 在十歲那年。

2. in trouble 惹上麻煩。

3. in trouble with the police 惹上警方。

4. steal（*v.*）偷竊。

5. home for bad children（收容問題少年的）少年之家。

6. boys' prison 少年監獄。

7. men's prison 成人監獄。

8. for the first time 第一次、首度。

9. Kenmore was in prison for seven of the next ten years. 接下來十年之中，肯摩爾坐了七年牢。

10. thief（*n.*）小偷、賊。

11. interesting（*adj.*）有趣的。

12. The police always caught him. 警方永遠都能逮到他。

13. con man 騙子。

14. trick（*n.*）欺詐、騙術。

15. up to 直至。

16. The police never caught him, up to the age of 50. 到他五十歲那年，警方才逮到他。

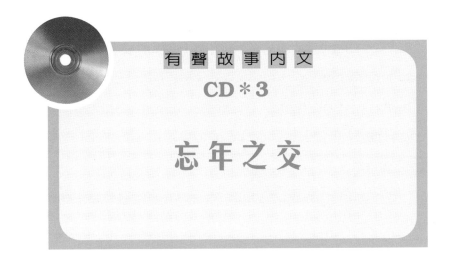

有聲故事內文
CD＊3

忘年之交

Tremaine and Kenmore were soon friends.

The other men in the prison were **surprised**. Tremaine was from a good family, and from the best schools, and from **Harvard University**. There was a great difference between him and Kenmore. But Kenmore had **promise**. Tremaine saw that.

For one thing, the young man didn't look like a thief. He didn't look like a boy from an orphanage. And Kenmore wasn't really **stupid**. Tremaine saw that too. The young man was **smart**.

For three years, Tremaine was Kenmore's teacher. Kenmore read books. And Tremaine helped him understand them. Tremaine taught Kenmore to speak good English. And he taught him the tricks of a con man.

Tremaine liked Kenmore, but that was not the only reason for his trouble.

He was old, and he needed help with his tricks. Kenmore understood Tremaine's reason, and he wanted to learn. He wanted to be a con man. But he never worked with Tremaine.

■ 內文提示：

1. surprise（v.）驚訝。

2. Harvard University　哈佛大學：美國名校，位於麻州劍橋，鄰近波士頓。

3. There was a great difference between him and Kenmore. 他和肯摩爾彼此之間有很大的差異。

4. promise（*n.*）前途、希望、前景。

5. For one thing, the young man didn't look like a thief. 其中一點是，這小子看起來不像小偷。

6. stupid（*adj.*）愚笨的、蠢的。

7. smart（*adj.*）聰明的、伶俐的。

8. trouble（*n.*）麻煩、煩勞、辛苦。

9. that was not the only reason for his trouble 他這麼費心，並非只為了這個原因。

▲在獄中，史丹利教他讀書，說一口漂亮的英文。

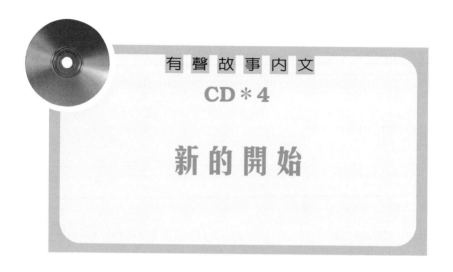

有 聲 故 事 內 文

CD＊4

新 的 開 始

"You're going to leave prison next month," the old man said one day. "Get a good **apartment** for us on a good street in Boston, and wait for me. You can use my money. I'll give you a **check**."

Two days after that, the old con man died **suddenly** in the prison. Kenmore was very sad.

Kenmore left prison. But this was a new James Kenmore. This was not just an unsuccessful thief.

The new James Kenmore knew a lot about the world. He spoke good English. And he knew all the

▲出獄後，他走在波士頓街頭，想著未來的路該如何走。

tricks of the con man.

But he had to think.

"I know the tricks," he thought. "I've learned them from Stanley Tremaine. But can I use them? I've always been a failure. Can I be a successful con man?"

He had Tremaine's money. It was only eight hundred dollars, but it gave Kenmore time to **think about** things. He took a small apartment on a good street. He bought some clothes. Then, for a month, he just lived **quietly**. He wanted to think.

"The trouble is," he thought, "I'm afraid. Without Tremaine, I'm **afraid** to try a real trick. I need **experience**. Can I get people to **trust** me?"

內文提示：

1. apartment（*n.*）公寓。

2. check（*n.*）支票。

3. suddenly（*adv.*）突然間。

4. I've always been a failure. 我一直都是個失敗者。

5. think about 思考、考慮。

6. quietly（*adv.*）靜靜地。

7. afraid（*adj.*）害怕的。

8. experience（*n.*）經驗。

9. trust（*v.*）相信、信任。

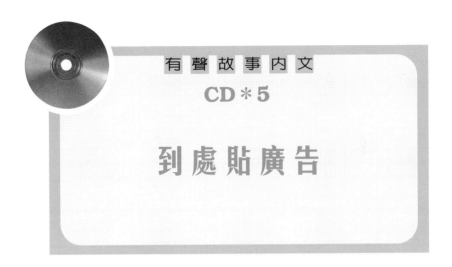

到處貼廣告

He remembered some words of Stanley Tremaine: "People trust psychics—but a lot of psychics are really con men. They pretend to help people, but they are really trying to learn facts about them. Then they use the facts to get money from those people."

Kenmore thought about that. "Maybe I can pretend to be a psychic," he thought. "I'll be careful, and it will be good experience."

In Boston, people often put up advertisements

▲他在波士頓市區到處貼靈媒廣告。

around town—on lampposts, telephone poles and trees. They write their advertisements—things to buy or sell—on a piece of paper and tape these signs to the lampposts.

"I'll put signs up around town," Kenmore thought.

He thought carefully about the words for his signs. Then he copied them on pieces of paper, and he

▲他整天坐在公寓裡等人家打電話來。

put them up all around town.

There wasn't any result.

His telephone didn't ring. He put more signs up.
He waited in his apartment all day. He sat near the
telephone. No result.

It didn't ring.

■ 內 文 提 示 ：

1. pretend（*v.*）假裝。

2. fact（*n.*）真相、事實。

3. advertisement（*n.*）廣告。

4. put up advertisements around town　在城裡四處張貼廣告。

5. lamppost（*n.*）燈柱。

6. telephone pole　電話桿。

7. a piece of paper　一張紙。

8. tape（*v.*）用膠帶黏牢。

9. sign（*n.*）招牌、告示。

10. There wasn't any result. 沒有任何結果。

11. His telephone didn't ring. 沒人打電話來。

12. He waited in his apartment all day. 他整天都在公寓裡等待。

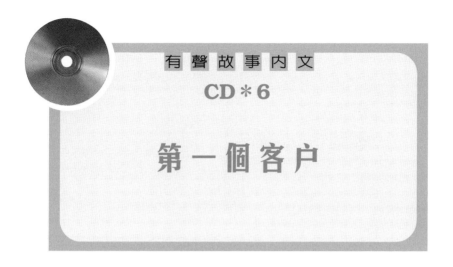

有聲故事內文
CD * 6

第一個客戶

"I'm near the end of Stanley Tremaine's money," he thought. "Am I going to have to steal things again? I wanted to be a con man, not a stupid thief. I have to try again."

He made more signs and put them up. He waited beside the telephone. After two days, it rang. A woman's voice said, "I saw your advertisement. Can I come to see you? Now?"

James Kenmore, psychic, had his first **client**.

It was really very easy. The woman was going to

▲終於有第一個客戶上門來。

start a new job. She wanted to know: "Will I be happy in the job?"

Kenmore talked to her for an hour. She told him a lot about her life and her **likes**. "She *will* like the job," he thought. But it was only a **guess**. He pretended to go into a **trance**. When he "came out" of the trance, he told her: "You'll love the job. It's just right for you."

She happily paid ten dollars.

A month after that, she sent him a check for another fifty dollars. "My job's very, very good," her letter said. "I'm really happy in it."

Kenmore was surprised. A lot of money, so easily! Just for a good guess!

內 文 提 示 ：

1. I'm near the end of Stanley Tremaine's money. 我快要把史丹利‧崔曼的錢用光了。

2. Am I going to have to steal again? 難道我又得去做小偷了嗎？

3. client（n.）客戶、客人。

4. She told him a lot about her life and her likes. 她告訴他許多關於自己生平的事以及她喜歡的事物。

5. likes（n. pl.）喜愛的事物，用複數形；厭惡的事物是dislikes，例句：

He made a list of his likes and dislikes. 他列出他喜歡和不喜歡的東西。

6. guess（*n.*）推測、猜想。

7. trance（*n.*）恍惚、昏迷狀態。

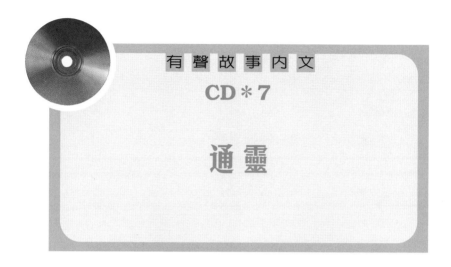

He put up his signs again.

Another client soon arrived—a man. His wife was dead, and he was very unhappy. Kenmore made another guess. "He wants a **message** from his dead wife," he thought.

He talked to the man for an hour. He **learned** a lot about the dead wife. Then he "went into a trance". He pretended to hear the dead wife. He spoke for her. The man wanted to hear a message, and Kenmore gave him the right message.

▲他又到處貼廣告。

The man heard the words and cried. He was very happy. He gave Kenmore fifty dollars.

"I'll come back soon for another message from her," he said.

For the next year, James Kenmore, psychic, was successful.

He **put advertisements in the newspapers**, and the newspaper advertisements brought clients. His old clients sent him new clients. He didn't always please a client. But after his mistakes, clients still gave him money. And he didn't often make a mistake.

He really helped the client. Not because he saw through time and space. But just because he understood things and the client didn't. A lot of people only wanted to talk about their troubles. Kenmore had a good face and the right voice for them.

內文提示：

1. message (*n.*) 信息。

2. learn (*v.*) 聽說、獲悉、知道。

3. He learned a lot about the dead wife. 他知道了許多關於這個亡妻的事。

4. He spoke for her. 他代她發言。

5. put advertisements in the newspapers 在報上登廣告。

6. He didn't always please a client. 他並不是每一次都能夠讓客戶滿意。

7. Kenmore had a good face and the right voice for them. 肯摩爾對他們，神態親切，講話的口吻也恰如其分。

有聲故事內文
CD * 8

遺失的手槍

Then a strange thing happened. One day a man came to ask Kenmore about an old gun.

"Who stole it?" he wanted to know. "Who was the thief? Where is the gun? The police have tried to find it, but they haven't been successful. I want the gun: it's very old—from George Washington's time—and my dead father gave it to me."

Kenmore didn't like the case. With cases of this kind he was nearly always a failure. He liked to make a clever guess, but guesses didn't work in cases of

▲誰偷走了那把槍？

this kind. But he didn't want to say that.

He told the man: "I'll try to help you."

He closed his eyes. It happened then—the strange thing. A bell rang in his head. It was a quiet sound, soft and strange and far away. It rang—and pictures came into his head. He started to speak:

"I can see it, I can see your old gun. Yes—but it isn't clear. I can't see it clearly. The shape changes—

it changes all the time. Oh! That's it! It's in water. It's under some water. And it's not far away."

"Not far away from here?" the man asked.

"Yes—no. Not far from here. It's not far away from you—from your house. It's less than half a mile from your house, and it's under water. And—that's all, that's all."

内文提示：

1. Who stole it? 誰偷走那把槍？

2. George Washington 喬治・華盛頓：美國國父。

3. from George Washington's time 從華盛頓時代留下的。

4. With cases of this kind he was nearly always a failure. 碰上這類案子他幾乎都是失敗的。

5. A bell rang in his head. 他的腦海裡響起一陣鈴聲。

6. pictures came into his head　他腦海裡出現一些影像。

7. The shape changes—it changes all the time.　形狀變來變去，一直在變。

8. Oh! That's it. 噢，是了！

9. It's in water. 它在水裡。

10. It's under some water. 沈在水底下。

11. Not far away from here? 離這裡不遠嗎？

12. It's less than half a mile from your house. 離你家不到半英里。

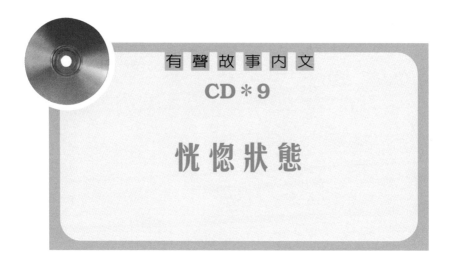

有聲故事內文
CD＊9

恍 惚 狀 態

Kenmore tried to open his eyes. But the world went black. He fainted.

After a while, the light came back. He opened his eyes and saw his client.

The man asked, "Are you all right?"

"Yes—yes, I'm all right."

"But you fainted. Does that always happen?"

"Well—no. Not always. But I'm all right now. Was it a long time—my faint?"

"No. Maybe a minute."

▲他陷入恍惚狀態，世界變成一片黑暗。

"Oh."

Kenmore tried to remember his words. But he was not successful. So he asked: "Did I help you?"

"Can't you remember?"

"No, I—I never can. That is, I never remember my words—in a trance."

"Well, you said, 'I can see your old gun. It's in water.' That's not right."

Kenmore thought, "No, it can't be right."

But he didn't say that.

He said: "Maybe it *is* right. I'm often right. Where did I tell you to look?"

The man sighed unhappily.

"You didn't tell me. Just: it's under water and not far away from my house. Who steals an old gun and puts it in water?"

■ 內 文 提 示 ：

1. the world went black 世界變成一片黑暗。

2. faint （*v. & n.*）昏倒。

3. after a while 過了一會兒。

4. Where did I tell you to look? 我有告訴你到哪裡去 找嗎？

5. sigh （*v.*）嘆氣。

有聲故事內文

CD * 10

池塘深處

Kenmore didn't know the answer. The man sighed again.

"There is a **pond** near my house. We'll **look in** that, but... Well, what do I have to pay?"

"I don't want any money," Kenmore said quickly. "Maybe you'll find your gun in the pond. Then you can send me a check. I'm not going to **ask for** it."

The man left. He was not very happy. Then Kenmore thought about it.

▲恍惚中他看到那把槍，沉在水底深處。

"That was strange! Why did I faint? Am I sick? That strange bell sound. Do I have to go to the doctor? And why did I say 'Maybe you'll find your gun in the pond?' Who steals an old gun and then throws it in a pond?"

The next day, Kenmore knew the answer to that question. The client came back to see him. He was very excited.

"I found my gun!" he cried. "It was in the pond

near my house. And there wasn't a thief. My little son took it. He just wanted to play with it, but he dropped it in the pond. And then he was afraid, and he didn't tell us."

Kenmore was surprised. But the client went on:

"You're a real psychic. You're wonderful. I'll tell all my friends about you. Please take this."

And he gave Kenmore two hundred dollars.

內 文 提 示 ：

1. pond（*n.*）池塘。

2. look in 看一下。

3. ask for 要求。

4. That strange bell sound. 那陣奇異的鈴聲。

5. Do I have to go to the doctor? 我要不要去看醫生？

6. excited（*adj.*）興奮的、激動的。

7. play with 玩弄、把玩。

8. go on 繼續下去。

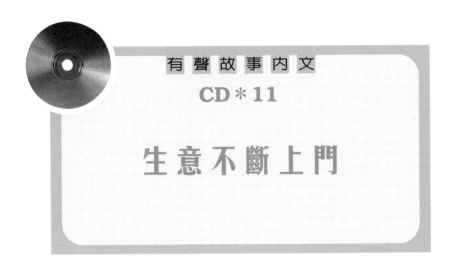

生意不斷上門

He left, and then Kenmore started to think. He wasn't happy.

Two hundred dollars was fine, but—what did it mean? "It's all right to be a con man," he thought, "but this is different."

He didn't want to be a real psychic—or wonderful. He was afraid.

But in three months it didn't happen again.

Kenmore had a lot of clients. With some he was successful. With others he wasn't. But he only lis-

▲做靈媒，賺錢居然如此容易。

tened and made guesses—good ones or bad ones.

"Maybe," he thought, "it was just the one strange dream. I'm not really a psychic. It's all right."

Then one day his **doorbell** rang. He went to the door and opened it. A tall man stood there.

"Mr. Kenmore?"

"Yes."

"I'm **Detective** Colson of the **Boston Police**

Department."

A **policeman**!

Kenmore didn't like the police. "But things are different now," he thought, "I'm not a thief. They can't send me to prison for this psychic business."

He asked, "What can I do for you, Detective Colson?"

"You know a Mr. Sargent, don't you? A Mr. Ralph Sargent?"

內 文 提 示 ：

1. doorbell （*n.*）門鈴。

2. detective （*n.*）刑警。

3. Boston Police Department 波士頓警察局。

4. policeman （*n.*）警察。

5. But things are different now. 然而現在情況已經不一樣了。

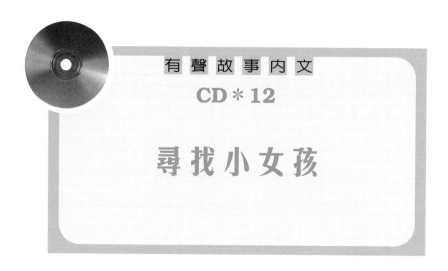

Yes, Kenmore knew him. Ralph Sargent was the man with the old gun.

"I do," said Kenmore. "I helped him at one time."

"I know. He talks about it a lot. He lives in the house next door to me."

"Really?"

"Well, now—I don't think—er—people don't see through time and space—you—you understand—"

Kenmore did understand. The detective wanted help.

▲警察上門來找他。

"I understand. You have a problem?"

"Yes, I *do* have a problem." He looked very serious. "She's gone. Just gone! We can't find her. A little girl. And I thought—well, I thought... Can I tell you
about it?"

"Please do. Come in and sit down."

But Kenmore was not happy about it. "The
police can't find her, so who can? I can't be success-

▲警方四處尋找一個失蹤的小女孩，希望他能幫上忙。

ful. This is bad. I didn't want the police to know about me."

But he had to listen. Detective Colson told him about the case.

Kenmore understood easily, but he asked some questions: "The little girl went out to buy some candy. Is that right? She never returned home. The police have **looked for** her for a week? You—"

■ 內 文 提 示 ：

1. at one time 一度、曾經。

2. talk about 談論。

3. He lives in the house next door to me. 他住在我家
   隔壁。

4. He looked very serious. 他看起來神情嚴肅。

5. She's gone. Just gone! 她不見了，就這麼不見了！

6. look for 尋找。

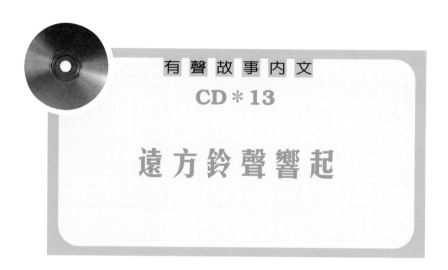

有 聲 故 事 內 文

CD * 13

遠方鈴聲響起

But then he stopped. He heard it—the little far-away bell rang in his head. He was surprised—and afraid.

The detective asked: "Mr. Kenmore? Are you all right?"

Kenmore closed his eyes. Pictures came to him. He began to talk:

"Yes—yes, I can see—Oh! She—she's in the dark. The little girl is in the dark. But there's light—far away. It's a tunnel. She's in a dark tunnel. And she's—she's dead. Oh... she's dead! The little girl is dead!"

Kenmore began to cry.

The detective was excited. He asked:

"And who did it? Mr. Kenmore, can you tell me that? Who *killed* her?"

Kenmore began: "No, I—"

But then it rang again—the faraway bell. He

▲他看到小女孩躺在隧道裡。

said:

"I see a man—a man in a car—no, a van. It's a small blue and white van. That's it, Detective Colson. Find that van, and then you'll—you'll have him. He did it—killed the little girl. And that's all—that's all—oh!"

And the world went black for James Kenmore.

內文提示：

1. faraway（*adj.*）遙遠的。

2. tunnel（*n.*）隧道。

3. van（*n.*）廂形車。

4. you'll have him 你會逮到他。

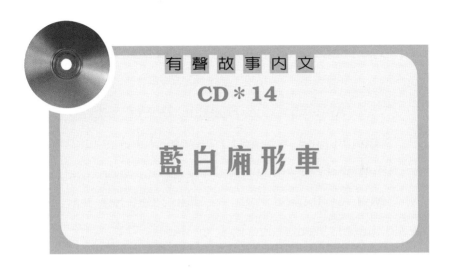

有聲故事內文
CD＊14

藍白廂形車

He opened his eyes. He was on his back on the floor. There was a serious look on the detective's face. Kenmore asked:

"What happened?"

"You fainted. Ralph—Mr. Sargent—told me about that. Are you all right?"

"Yes, thank you.—Did I say—did I help?"

"You really don't remember?"

"No. I—I heard it—the bell—and then—well, what did I say?"

"You spoke about a tunnel—and a blue and white van."

"I see. And what does it mean? Does it help?"

"I don't know. We did find a tunnel, but—"

"But what?"

"Well, we looked in it. We didn't find her. It was an old tunnel. We have to look again."

▲他從昏迷中醒過來，完全不知道自己發生了什麼事、說過什麼話。

In three hours, the first result came. The police found the body of the little girl. It was under the ground in the tunnel. After another week, they caught the man with the blue and white van. He was a mailman. He drove a mailman's blue and white van.

Detective Colson was really surprised. "It's wonderful," he told Kenmore. He brought him a letter of thanks from the Chief of the Boston Police.

"Look," Colson said, "this case was in the newspapers, and some reporters want to know about it. Can I tell them about you? —about your help?"

"All right," Kenmore said. And he answered the reporters' questions. But he was surprised by the results. There were stories about him in all the newspapers. And pictures. He was on television. In all parts of the country people talked about him.

■ 内 文 提 示 ：

1. He was on his back on the floor. 他躺在地板上。

2. I see. 我知道了。

3. result（*n.*）結果、成績。

4. the first result came 有了第一項成果。

5. under the ground 在地底下。

6. mailman（*n.*）郵差。

7. a letter of thanks 一封感謝函。

8. the Chief of the Boston Police 波士頓警察局局長。

9. This case was in the newspapers. 報紙報導了這樁案子。

10. reporter（*n.*）記者。

11. In all parts of the country people talked about him. 全國各地的人都在談論他。

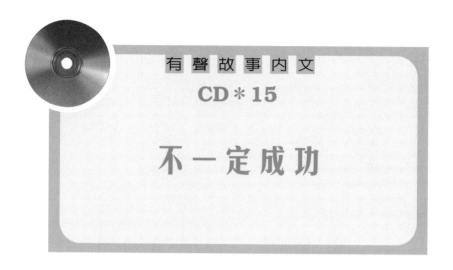

不 一 定 成 功

After that he was *very* successful.

People wrote to him from all parts of the world. Nearly all the letters asked for help.

Rich people wanted to give him a lot of money for a visit. Crowds of people came to his apartment, so he had to move. He didn't tell people the address of his new home, but he took an office on Tremont Street. He worked there every day, and he made a lot of money. His receptionist asked rich people for a very big fee. But he didn't see only rich people. Poor

▲肯摩爾一舉成名，客戶紛紛上門來。

people came to him, and he tried to help them, too. He didn't ask poor people for a fee.

People of all kinds trusted Kenmore. But he knew one thing, and they didn't: he was not really a wonderful psychic.

From time to time he heard the faraway bell, and then—only then—he knew the real answers.

He didn't hear it often.

At other times he just pretended to go into a trance. He made a guess. And he was often wrong.

Then the clients were angry. They wrote angry letters to the newspapers. "It is a trick," they said.

But then he heard his bell again. He found the answer to a very hard problem, and then the newspapers told the story, and he was famous again. Clients came in large numbers.

內 文 提 示 ：

1. ask for help　請求幫助、求援。
2. crowds of people　成群的人。
3. fee（*n.*）費用。
4. people of all kinds　各式各樣的人。
5. from time to time　有時候。
6. in large numbers　大量、大批。
7. Clients came in large numbers.　大批客戶紛紛上門來。

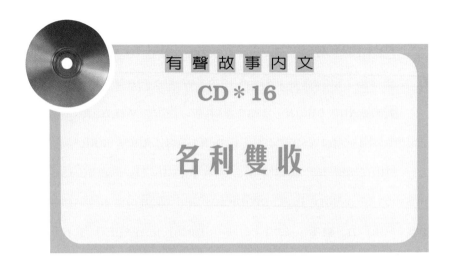

名利雙收

After five years, Kenmore was a rich man. He was the friend of famous and great people. The boy from a world of orphanages and prisons was happy in the houses of the great.

One of his clients was a senator. Kenmore helped him with an easy problem. The senator was very happy, and he asked Kenmore to visit his home. There Kenmore met the senator's daughter. A year after that, she and Kenmore were man and wife.

The boy from the orphanage had a senator's

daughter for his wife.

He was Stanley Tremaine's greatest success.

Kenmore loved his wife. He did not want to pretend to her. So he told her about his life—or—he told her a lot of it.

She knew these things: his mother left him and he grew up in an orphanage; he was very poor for

▲孤兒出身的肯摩爾娶了參議員的千金為妻。

years. But he didn't want to tell her about prison.

"Was I really in prison?" he thought. "Here I am, with a beautiful house, a big car, famous friends, a happy family. Am I really that thief out of prison? I'm different now. I'm a kind and good man—all my friends say that. They're right, aren't they? The old Jimmy Kenmore is dead."

▲肯摩爾名利雙收。

■ 內 文 提 示 ：

1. senator（*n.*）參議員。

2. man and wife　夫妻。

3. She and Kenmore were man and wife. 她和肯摩爾結為夫妻。

4. The boy from the orphanage had a senator's daughter for his wife. 孤兒院出身的小伙子娶了參議員的千金。

5. greatest success　最大的成就。

6. Was I really in prison? 我真的坐過牢嗎？

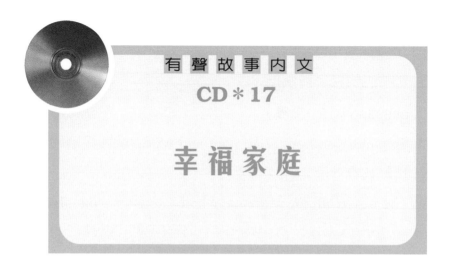

有 聲 故 事 內 文

CD * 17

幸 福 家 庭

For ten years, the Kenmores were happy. They had two children—boys. Kenmore loved them deeply. They were smart and good. It was a fine life.

One day, Mike Colson visited Kenmore's office.

Colson—you remember—brought Kenmore his first big case.

Inspector—not Detective now—Colson was Kenmore's friend. He often asked Kenmore for help. Sometimes Kenmore was successful with Colson's problems. Sometimes not.

▲肯摩爾與警探成為好朋友，他幫助警方解決許多懸案。

Colson knew about Kenmore's faraway bell. He called it Kenmore's "gift". He didn't try to understand his friend's power.

Colson had another problem.

It was a murder case. He told Kenmore about it and then asked, "Can you help us, Jimmy?"

Kenmore closed his eyes. But he didn't hear his faraway bell. He opened his eyes again.

"No. I can't help, Mike."

Inspector Colson sighed.

He asked: "You're not losing it, are you? Your gift?"

"Oh—no! It doesn't always work. You know that."

"Yes—but it hasn't worked for a year this time." Colson sighed again.

He really liked Kenmore, and he was sad about Kenmore's "gift".

"Hasn't it?"

"The last time was the Baker case. You found the answer to that murder for me. But that was last year."

"Was it?"

"Yes."

1. the Kenmores 肯摩爾一家人。

2. inspector （*n.*）巡官。

3. detective （*n.*）刑警。

4. gift （*n.*）天賦。

5. a murder case　一件謀殺案。

6. Jimmy （*n.*）James 的小名。

7. work （*v.*）運轉、有效、發揮作用。

8. It doesn't always work. 不一定每次都會成功。

9. the Baker case　貝克案件：貝克是指這樁案子的主
要受害人或加害人的姓氏。

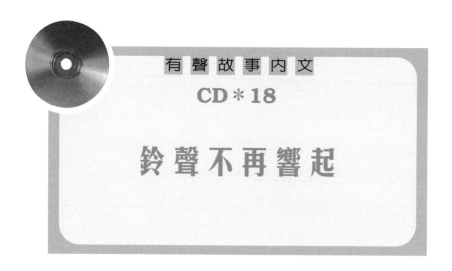

有聲故事內文

CD＊18

鈴聲不再響起

Colson went, and Kenmore looked at his papers.

"Colson's right," he thought. "I haven't heard it for fourteen months. That's a long time. Have I lost it? Will it never **come back**? What will happen then?"

Another year. And still Kenmore didn't hear his bell.

He was really afraid.

Clients still came to see him, but not in large numbers. Kenmore knew the reason.

"Advertisements don't bring many clients. Rich

clients come only to famous psychics. I have to be successful with *hard* problems. And for that I need my bell. Will I never hear it again?"

One evening, the Kenmores were the hosts at a dinner party. Mike Colson was there. There was a famous reporter. And there were other rich and famous people. Fourteen sat down to dinner.

It was a fine dinner party. The food was good, and the talk was good too. Near the end of the meal, the talk turned to murders. There was the case of Sarah Collins in the newspapers. Sarah Collins was a Boston girl. The police found her body beside the road fifty miles from Boston. The reporter asked Colson about the murder.

"Do you know anything about the case, Inspector?"

"Yes, I do," Colson answered. "It's my case."

內 文 提 示 ：

1. come back 回來、恢復。

2. Another year. 又過了一年。

3. host（*n.*）（宴會等的）主人。

4. dinner party 晚宴。

5. murder（*n.*）謀殺、謀殺案。

6. Near the end of the meal, the talk turned to murders. 用餐接近尾聲時，話題轉到謀殺。

7. beside the road 在路邊。

8. It's my case. 那是我經辦的案子。

▲有時候他失去了靈媒的「天賦」。

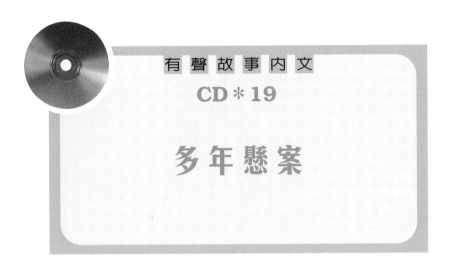

有聲故事內文

CD＊19

多年懸案

"Will you find the murderer?"

"I don't know. Maybe we won't."

The other people were surprised. One asked:

"But you'll try—you won't stop?"

"Oh, yes. We'll try. But—we don't often find the answer in cases of this kind." Then the inspector smiled at Kenmore. "Maybe Jimmy will help us. He always helped us with hard problems in the old days."

A woman asked: "But don't you always catch murderers?"

▲在晚宴上，眾人的話題轉到謀殺案。

"No. Not always."

"But what do you do? Just forget about them?"

Colson sighed.

"Not really. We keep them **on the books**. But there are a lot of old cases. The police can't try to find the answers year after year."

"But do you never find the answers to a *lot* of murders?"

"Yes, we have a lot of failures. You see, some murders are easy. We call them 'family' murders. The murderer is in the **victim**'s family. Or he lives in or near the victim's house. So the victim knew the murderer. We nearly always find the murderer in cases of that kind. But there is another kind. The murderer and the victim are **strangers**. They might only meet that one time. And then the murder happens. Maybe Sarah Collins and her murderer were strangers."

■ **內文提示**：

1. murderer（*n.*）兇手。

2. We'll try. 我們會試試看。

3. in the old days 往昔、從前。

4. But don't you always catch murderers? 但是你們不是總會逮到兇手嗎？

5. But what do you do? Just forget about them? 那麼你們怎麼辦？就這樣算了嗎？

6. on the books 有記載、有案可查。

7. We keep them on the books. 我們把這些案子留在檔案裡。

8. victim（*n.*）受害人。

9. The murderer is in the victim's family. 兇手是被害人的親人。

10. stranger（*n.*）陌生人。

11. The murderer and the victim are strangers. 兇手和被害人互不相識。

12. They might only meet that one time. 他們也許只見過那一次。

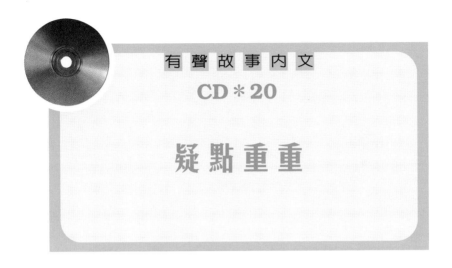

有 聲 故 事 內 文

CD * 20

疑 點 重 重

"Did you get a lot of cases of that kind?"

"Yes," said Colson. "And often we don't catch the murderer. My first case was a murder of that kind. I was twenty then."

"And you've never found the murderer?"

"No. And we won't now. It was a strange case. The victim was a policeman—a Boston police inspector, like me today."

This was interesting to all the people at the dinner party. They asked Inspector Colson to tell them

▲警探談起他二十歲那年發生的一樁奇怪的案子。

about the case.

"Well, the inspector died very suddenly. The murderer hit him on the head with an **iron bar**. It happened in the **living room** of his house."

The reporter said, "I remember that case. But you said, 'It was a strange case.' Why?"

"I'll tell you. The police found the inspector with his gun in his hand. But all its six **shots** were still in

▲被害人也是個警探。

the gun. The murderer hit him from the front—we know that—but the inspector never fired. That doesn't happen to good policemen. Why didn't he fire? A murderer hit him from in front with an iron bar, and he just stood there with a gun in his hand and didn't fire. Why? And who did it?"

"Didn't you make a guess?"

內文提示：

1. a strange case 一樁奇怪的案子。

2. iron bar 鐵棒。

3. living room 客廳。

4. shot（n.）一發子彈。

5. But all its six shots were still in the gun. 但是手槍裡的六發子彈都還在。

6. front（n.）前面、正面。

7. The murderer hit him from the front. 兇手從正面襲擊他。

8. fire（v.）開火、開槍。

9. Why didn't he fire? 他為何不開槍？

有聲故事內文
CD＊21

閉上眼睛

"Yes. The inspector had a big case at that time. He was going out that night to catch a large gang. Maybe the gang knew that. Maybe they sent two or three men to murder him. But why didn't he use his gun? What was the trick? We don't know."

A man said, "Maybe it was just one desperate thief?"

"No. No. It's not just a thief's work. Inspector Nicholls had a gun in his hand. No, that murderer was very smart."

▲大家不能理解的是，為何他不開槍？

"Or very stupid," said James Kenmore.

They looked at him.

"What do you mean, Jimmy?" asked Inspector Colson.

Kenmore's eyes were shut. He sat very still in his chair. He said:

"I know—I can see—I can see it all."

Inspector Colson looked at him. The policeman

▲突然間，肯摩爾的遠方鈴聲又響起。

was excited. He asked:

"Jimmy? Has it come back? Your gift?"

"Yes—thank God. It *has* come back."

內 文 提 示 ：

1. gang（*n.*）幫派。

2. murder（*v.*）謀殺。

3. What was the trick? 搞什麼玩意？

4. desperate（*adj.*）不顧一切的、鋌而走險的。

5. work（*n.*）所做的事。

6. It's not just a thief's work. 這不會只是一名小偷幹的事。

7. still（*adj.*）靜止不動的。

8. He sat very still in his chair. 他坐在椅子上一動也不動。

9. I can see it all. 我全都看見了。

有聲故事內文
CD＊22

小賊

It was the name of the victim—Inspector Nicholls. That name brought the sound of the faraway bell.

"I'll be all right now." Kenmore knew. "I'll tell them all about it. And there's a reporter in the room. He'll write a story about it. I'll be famous again."

Then he forgot the party. He forgot Inspector Colson and the other people at his table. He forgot his wife and his home. He saw only that night—years back in time. He started to talk.

"Inspector Nicholls was very tired that night. He

wanted to catch the gang, and that meant work day and night. He had to go out again in an hour, but he needed sleep. He was the only person in the house, so he lay down in his living room. He turned out the light and slept." （註）

The picture in Kenmore's head was clear.

"I can see... A thief is moving across the inspector's garden. He's a young thief. He doesn't know the house. It's a policeman's house, but he doesn't know that. He just wants to steal money or silver. He moves near to the window. He has an iron bar—an iron bar to open the window. But the thief tries the window, and it moves.

He's surprised, but he opens it.

He goes through it into the room. He doesn't see the inspector in the dark room. And Nicholls is sleeping deeply, he doesn't hear the thief.

The thief has a flashlight. He shines it on a table

▲小賊想用鐵棒撬開窗子。

beside the wall near the window. He still doesn't see Nicholls, but he does see a silver box on the table. He goes to the table, puts his flashlight on it, and takes the silver box in his hands...

內文提示：

1. years back in time　時光往前推許多年。
2. work day and night　日以繼夜地工作。

3. turn out the light　關燈。

4. silver（*n.*）銀器。

5. flashlight（*n.*）手電筒。

6. shine（*v.*）照亮。

附註：肯摩爾敘述往事時，起初用的是過去式動詞時態，當他腦海中的影像愈來愈清晰，往事歷歷在目，如同發生在當下，他也就改成用現在式。

有聲故事內文

CD＊23

夢中醒來

"Suddenly Nicholls moves in his sleep.

What's that? The thief is surprised and afraid.

He drops the box and it makes a noise. Nicholls wakes up. Quickly and quietly he takes hold of his gun. He stands up and points the gun at the thief.

'Stand still! Don't move,' he says.

The thief stands still. He *can't* move. He's afraid—afraid!

'Turn around!' And the thief turns around.

He still has his iron bar, but his flashlight is on

▲警探用槍指住小賊，叫他站住。

the table. It's still shining, but it's pointing at the wall. The policeman and the thief can't see well. Nicholls can see a thing—it's the iron bar—in the thief's hand.

'Drop that!' The thief is going to drop it—but—"

內文提示：

1. wake up 醒來。

2. take hold of 握住、抓住。

3. point at 指向、對準。

4. Stand still! 站住！

5. Don't move. 不要動。

6. Turn around! 轉過身來！

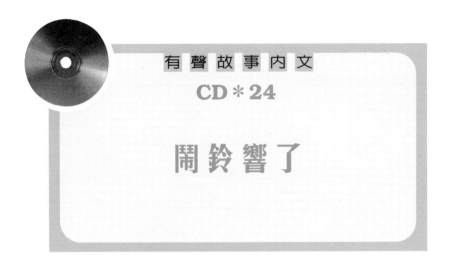

有 聲 故 事 內 文

CD＊24

鬧 鈴 響 了

Kenmore stopped. He heard it again.

The faraway bell. But why now? What—? And then he understood.

It was a bell, but it wasn't a faraway bell. It *was* a very small bell, and it was near. It was in Nicholls's watch. Policemen often have watches of that kind. Nicholls wanted to sleep for an hour, so he put the hand of his watch to ring the bell in an hour. This was the end of that hour, and the bell rang.

Kenmore spoke again. "The inspector is surprised. He looks down at his watch. He must stop it. He always stops the bell with his finger, so he touches the watch.

The gun's moving! It isn't pointing at the thief!

That's a mistake. The thief sees it. It's his only chance—a chance to get away—to stay out of prison—and he's desperate.

He brings his iron bar down on Nicholls' head.

▲他跑啊跑啊，衝出花園，衝到外面去。

He doesn't wait to see the result. He's afraid—afraid—afraid! He takes his flashlight and runs.

He runs.

He runs.

Through the garden. And away! "

■内文提示：

1. Nicholls wanted to sleep for an hour. 尼可斯想睡上一個鐘頭。

2. hand（*n.*）（鐘表的）指針。

3. He put the hand of his watch to ring the bell in an hour. 他把手表設在一小時後發出鈴響。

4. It's his only chance. 那是他唯一的機會。

5. get away 逃走。

6. stay out of prison 避免入獄。

7. He brings his iron bar down on Nicholls' head. 他揮舞鐵棒，敲在尼可斯的頭上。

寫下名字

Kenmore stopped again and sighed. His face was white, and there was a very sad look on it. He said:

"That thief wasn't a murderer. He was just young, and stupid—and afraid—desperately afraid. He—"

Inspector Colson was excited. "Jimmy! Who did it? Do you know? Who did it? And where can we find him?"

Kenmore didn't open his eyes. Slowly—very slowly—he said:

"Give me—a pencil—paper. I'll write it. I know."

They found a pencil and paper. They put the pencil into Kenmore's hand. Still with his eyes closed, he wrote. He wrote in large round letters—the letters of a child. He wrote slowly—slowly and sadly.

At the end, he said, "That's all. Oh!"

Then he fainted.

▲他在紙上寫下小賊的名字和地址。

地址及姓名

After a minute he opened his eyes. All their eyes were on him. What happened? Then he remembered. His bell! He heard it again. He was a real psychic again. He asked:

"Did I do it? Mike, did I do it?"

Inspector Colson's face was sad.

"Yes, Jimmy. You did it. You told us all about it."

"And the murderer? Did I tell you the murderer's name? Did I give you his address?"

Inspector Colson held up the paper with

Kenmore's message on it. "You wrote them, Jimmy. On this paper."

Kenmore sighed happily. "So I still have it—my gift. I haven't lost it."

"No, you haven't lost it, Jimmy."

"Well, tell me, Mike. What's on that paper? What did I write?"

Colson sighed deeply. Then he said:

"You wrote *this* address, Jimmy. And you wrote the name of the murderer. It's your name, Jimmy. It's James Kenmore."

內文提示 ：

1. All their eyes were on him. 他們的眼睛全都盯著他。

2. hold up 舉起、持起。

3. on this paper 在這張紙上。

4. What did I write? 我寫了什麼 ?

中英有聲解說
CD ＊ 27~35

中英有聲解說

Key words

CD ＊ 27

psychic 靈媒、通靈的人

receptionist 櫃檯人員、接待員

Cadillac 凱迪拉克

downtown 市區

orphanage 孤兒院

at the age of 10 在十歲那一年

prison 監獄

CD * 28

for the first time 第一次

con man 騙子

trick 騙術

Harvard University 哈佛大學

promise 有前途、有希望

apartment 公寓

CD * 29

experience 經驗

pretend 假裝

think about 考慮

advertisement 廣告

sign 招牌、告示

CD * 30

client 客戶、客人

trance 恍惚、昏迷狀態

message　信息

Not far away from here?　離這裡不遠嗎？

CD＊31

faint　昏倒

sigh　嘆氣

He looked very serious.　他看起來神情嚴肅。

tunnel　隧道

van　廂形車

CD＊32

reporter　記者

fee　費用

senator　參議員

CD＊33

inspector　巡官

detective　刑警

gift 天賦

host 主人

CD＊34

murder 謀殺

murderer 兇手

victim 受害人

stranger 陌生人

suddenly 突然間

CD＊35

gang 幫派

desperate 不顧一切的

work day and night 日以繼夜的工作

silver 銀器

shine 照亮

Turn around! 轉過身來！

靈 媒 的 故 事
The Psychic

字彙量：1200 字

這部以真實故事改編的有聲書，一共有26段。

你可以一口氣聽完，也可分段來聽，當然更可以躺著聽。然後作填空測驗，把括弧內遺漏掉的字（有的不只一個字）寫下，看看自己的聽力程度如何。解答附在每一組內文之後。

記住，先聽幾遍，再對照原文。

一開始不要先看內文，以免寵壞了耳朵，它就不管用了。

在後半部，由兩位中美老師仔細唸出單字及片語，複述重要的句子。尤其是單字以清晰的美語發音，並拼出字母，可幫助你記憶單字。只要多聽幾遍，你將很驚訝地發現，原來英文可以聽聽就會。

聽力小祕訣：至少先聽六遍以上，再翻開書來看。即使不能完全聽懂，也要讓耳朵熟悉英語的聲音與語調。

具戲劇和音效的臨場感，剛開始你也許不太適應，但只要多聽幾遍，耳朵熟能生巧，漸漸就能融會貫通。

學英文要像吃自助餐，不要老吃同一道菜，最好是各色好菜搭配著吃，這樣才不會吃膩。所以，建議你把家裡的幾套CD有聲書拿出來，替換著聽，一來避免聽膩了，二來英語更容易觸類旁通，聽力越練越好，會話也跟著進步。

倘若你的聽力不佳，聽不懂別人說的話，那要如何回答呢？恐怕是「答非所問」。所以要先會聽，就會說，也會寫。

聽有聲書，你會發現，學英語是多麼有趣的過程。你並不需要認識每一個單字，也不必完全聽懂所有的句子，就能輕鬆享受聽故事的樂趣。

聽 力 測 驗
CD＊1
公車上的棄兒

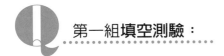

第一組**填空測驗**：

James Kenmore was a（**1.**　　　　　）.

People say: "A real psychic（**2.**　　　　）time and space." It is a strange power. Not many people really have that（**3.**　　　　）.

James Kenmore was a very successful psychic. Rich people paid a lot of money for his help. They came to his（**4.**　　　　）on Tremont Street. There they（**5.**　　　）to his（**6.**　　　），and the receptionist took them to his room. Brent had a big（**7.**　　　　）car. He lived in a beautiful house. He was 50 years old. He loved his wife and his two sons, and they loved him.

But Kenmore was not always successful. Oh, no. For the first 35 years of his life he was a (8.　　　　). He started life a failure. He started (9.　　　　) a father or a mother.

People found the baby James Kenmore on a Boston (10.　　　　). Maybe his mother (11.　　　　) him there? The bus carried people from (12.　　　　) Boston to Kenmore Square, so they gave that name to the baby. He (13.　　　　) in an orphanage—with 50 other children without mothers or fathers. The orphanage was 10 miles (14.　　　　) of Boston.

第一組測驗解答：

1. psychic　2. sees through　3. power　4. office
5. spoke　6. receptionist　7. Cadillac　8. failure

9. without   10. bus   11. left   12. downtown
13. grew up 14. outside

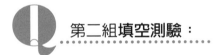 第二組**填空測驗**：

At the age of 10, James Kenmore was in trouble with the police. He stole things from stores. He had to go to a home for bad children.

（**1.**　　　　　）15, he stole a car. For this he had to go to a（**2.**　　　　）. At 19, he was in trouble with the police again, and he went to a men's prison（**3.**　　　　）. Why? Because he（**4.**　　　　）things from houses.

Kenmore was in prison for seven of the (5.   ) ten years. He went there for two years, and then two years again, and then three years. Between those times in prison he always started work in a (6.   ). But he didn't like his work, and he was soon in trouble again.

The life of a (7.   ) was interesting, and his job wasn't interesting. But he was not a smart thief. The police always (8.   ) him. At the age of 30, they caught him again, and he went to prison for five years. In prison he (9.   ) Stanley Tremaine.

Stanley Tremaine was a (10.   ). He got money from people by tricks. He was a smart con man. The police never caught him, up to the age of 50. Then he tried a very big trick. They caught him, and he went to prison for seven years.

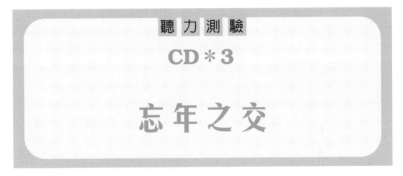

A 第二組測驗解答：

1. At the age of 2. boys' prison 3. for the first time
4. stole 5. next 6. real job 7. thief 8. caught
9. met 10. con man

聽 力 測 驗

CD ＊ 3

忘 年 之 交

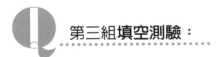

Q 第三組填空測驗：

Tremaine   and   Kenmore   were   soon
（1.   ）.

The other men in the prison were（2.   ）.
Tremaine was from a good family, and from the
best schools, and from（3.   ）University.

There was a great (4.   ) between him and Kenmore. But Kenmore had (5.   ). Tremaine saw that.

For one thing, the young man didn't (6.   ) a thief. He didn't look like a boy from an orphanage. And Kenmore wasn't really (7.   ). Tremaine saw that too. The young man was smart.

For three years, Tremaine was Kenmore's teacher. Kenmore read books. And Tremaine helped him understand them. Tremaine taught Kenmore to speak good English. And he taught him the tricks of a con man. Tremaine liked Kenmore, but that was not (8.   ) for his trouble.

He was old, and he needed help with his tricks. Kenmore understood Tremaine's reason, and he wanted to learn. He wanted to be a con man. But he never worked with Tremaine.

A 第三組測驗解答：

1. friends　2. surprised　3. Harvard　4. difference

5. promise　6. look like　7. stupid　8. the only reason

聽 力 測 驗

CD＊4

新 的 開 始

Q 第四組填空測驗：

　　"You're going to（1.　　　　　）prison next month," the old man said（2.　　　　　）. "Get a good（3.　　　　　）for us on a good street in Boston, and（4.　　　　　）me. You can use my money. I'll give you a（5.　　　　　）."

　　Two days after that, the old con man died suddenly in the prison. Kenmore was very sad.

Kenmore left prison. But this was a new James Kenmore. This was not just an (6.　　　　) thief.

The new James Kenmore knew a lot about the world. He spoke good English. And he knew all the tricks of the con man.

But he had to think.

"I know the tricks. I've learned them from Stanley Tremaine. But can I use them? I've always (7.　　　　) a failure. Can I be a successful con man?"

He had Tremaine's money. It was only eight hundred dollars, but it gave Kenmore time to (8.　　　　) things. He took a small apartment on a good street. He bought some clothes. Then, for a month, he just lived (9.　　　　). He wanted to think.

"The trouble is, I'm （10.　　　　）. Without Tremaine, I'm afraid to try a real trick. I need （11.　　　　）. Can I get people to trust me?"

第四組測驗解答：

1. leave　2. one day　3. apartment　4. wait for
5. check　6. unsuccessful　7. been　8. think about
9. quietly　10. afraid　11. experience

聽 力 測 驗

CD＊5

到 處 貼 廣 告

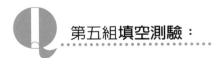

第五組填空測驗：

He（1.　　　　）some words of Stanley Tremaine: "People trust psychics—but a lot of psychics are really con men. They pretend to help people, but they are really trying to learn (2.   ) about them. Then they use the facts to get money from those people."

Kenmore thought about that. "Maybe I can pretend to be a psychic. I'll be (3.   ), and it will be good experience."

In Boston, people often (4.   ) advertisements around town—on (5.   ), telephone poles and trees. They write their (6.   ) —things to buy or sell—on a piece of paper and (7.   ) these signs to the lampposts.

"I'll put (8.   ) up around town."

He thought carefully about the words for his signs. Then he copied them on pieces of paper, and he put them up all around town.

There wasn't any result.

His telephone didn't （**9.** 　　　　　）. He put
more signs up. He waited in his apartment all day.
He sat near the telephone. No result.

It didn't ring.

第五組測驗解答：

1. remembered　**2.** facts　**3.** careful　**4.** put up
5. lampposts　**6.** advertisements　**7.** tape　**8.** signs
9. ring

聽 力 測 驗
CD＊6

第 一 個 客 户

第六組填空測驗：

"I'm near（**1.** 　　　　　）Stanley Tremaine's

money. Am I going to have to steal things again? I wanted to be a con man, not a stupid thief. I have to try again."

He made more signs and put them up. He waited (2.   ) the telephone. After two days, it rang. A woman's voice said, "I saw your advertisement. Can I come to see you? Now?"

James Kenmore, psychic, had his first (3.   ).

It was really very easy. The woman was going to start a new job. She wanted to know: "Will I be happy in the job?"

Kenmore talked to her (4.   ) . She told him a lot about her life and her (5.   ) . "She will like the job," he thought. But it was only a (6.   ) . He pretended to go into (7.   ) . When he "came out" of the trance, he told her: "You'll love the job. It's just right for you."

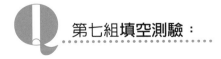

Listening Test

聽力測驗 7

She (8.   ) paid ten dollars.

A month after that, she sent him a check for another fifty dollars. "My job's very, very good," her letter said. "I'm really happy in it."

Kenmore was surprised. A lot of money, so (9.   )! Just for a good guess!

A 第六組**測驗解答**：

1. the end of 2. beside 3. client 4. for an hour
5. likes 6. guess 7. a trance 8. happily 9. easily

聽 力 測 驗
CD * 7
通 靈

Q 第七組**填空測驗**：

He put up his signs again.

Another client soon arrived—a man. His wife was dead, and he was very unhappy. Kenmore made another guess. "He wants a (1.   ) from his dead wife," he thought.

He talked to the man for an hour. He learned a lot about the dead wife. Then he "went into a trance". He pretended to hear the dead wife. He spoke for her. The man wanted to hear a message, and Kenmore gave him the right message.

The man (2.   ) the words and cried. He was very happy. He gave Kenmore fifty dollars.

"I'll come back soon for another message from her," he said.

For the next year, James Kenmore, psychic, was successful.

He put advertisements in the newspapers, and the newspaper advertisements (3.   )

clients. His old clients sent him new clients. He didn't always (**4.**   ) a client. But after his (**5.**   ), clients still gave him money. And he didn't often make a mistake.

He really helped the client. Not because he saw through time and space. But just because he understood things and the client didn't. A lot of people only wanted to talk about their (**6.**   ). Kenmore had a good face and the right voice for them.

第七組測驗解答：

1. message **2.** heard **3.** brought **4.** please
5. mistakes **6.** troubles

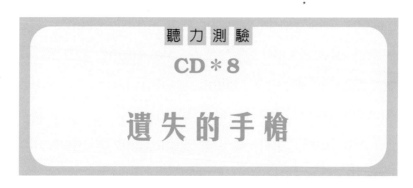

聽 力 測 驗

CD ＊ 8

遺 失 的 手 槍

第八組**填空測驗**：

Then a strange thing happened. One day a man came to ask Kenmore about an old gun.

"Who stole it? Who was the thief? Where is the gun? The police have tried to find it, but they haven't been successful. I want the gun: it's very old—from George Washington's time—and my dead father gave it to me."

Kenmore didn't like the case. With cases of this kind he was (1.   ) always a failure. He liked to make a (2.   ) guess, but guesses didn't work in cases of this kind. But he didn't want to say that.

He told the man: "I'll try to help you."

He closed his eyes. It (3.   ) then— the strange thing. A bell rang in his head. It was a quiet sound, (4.   ) and strange and far away. It rang and pictures came into his head. He started to speak:

"I can see it, I can see your old gun. Yes— but it isn't clear. I can't see it clearly. The (5.   ) changes— it changes (6.   ). Oh! That's it! It's in water. It's under (7.   ) water. And it's not far away."

"Not (8.   ) from here?"

"Yes—no. Not far from here. It's not far away from you—from your house. It's (9.   ) half a mile from your house, and it's under water. And—that's all, that's all."

第八組**測驗解答**：

1. nearly 2. clever 3. happened 4. soft 5. shape

6. all the time 7. some 8. far away 9. less than

聽 力 測 驗

CD＊9

恍 惚 狀 態

第九組**填空測驗**：

Kenmore tried to open his eyes. But the world

（1.   ）. He fainted.

After a while, the light came back. He opened his eyes and saw his client.

The man asked, "Are you all right?"

"Yes—yes, I'm (2.   )."

"But you fainted. Does that always happen?"

"Well—no. Not always. But I'm all right now. Was it a long time—my (3.   )?"

"No. Maybe a minute."

"Oh."

Kenmore tried to remember his (4.   ). But he was not successful. So he asked: "Did I help you?"

"Can't you remember?"

"No, I—I never can. That is, I never remember my words—in a trance."

"Well, you said, 'I can see your old gun. It's in water.' That's not right."

Kenmore thought, "No, it can't be right."

But he didn't say that.

He said: "Maybe it is right. I'm often right. Where did I tell you to look?"

The man sighed unhappily.

"You didn't tell me. Just: it's (**5.**   )
and not far away from my house. Who steals an old
gun and puts it in water?"

 第九組測驗解答：

1. went black   **2.** all right   **3.** faint   **4.** words
5. under water

聽 力 測 驗

CD＊10

池塘深處

 第十組填空測驗：

Kenmore didn't know the answer. The man

（1.　　　　　）again.

"There is a （2.　　　　）near my house. We'll look in that, but... Well, what do I have to pay?"

"I don't want any money. Maybe you'll find your gun in the pond. Then you can send me a check. I'm not going to ask for it."

The man left. He was not very happy. Then Kenmore thought about it.

"That was strange! Why did I faint? Am I （3.　　　　）? That strange bell （4.　　　　）. Do I have to go to the doctor? And why did I say 'Maybe you'll find your gun in the pond?' Who steals an old gun and then （5.　　　　）it in a pond?"

The next day, Kenmore knew the answer to that question. The client came back to see him. He was very excited.

"I found my gun! It was in the pond near my house. And there wasn't a thief. My (**6.**   ) took it. He just wanted to play with it, but he (**7.**   ) it in the pond. And then he was afraid, and he didn't tell us."

Kenmore was surprised. But the client went on:

"You're a real psychic. You're (**8.**   ). I'll tell all my friends about you. Please take this."

And he gave Kenmore two hundred dollars.

A 第十組測驗解答：

1. sighed **2.** pond **3.** sick **4.** sound **5.** throws
6. little son **7.** dropped **8.** wonderful

Listening Test
聽力測驗 11

聽 力 測 驗

CD ✳ 11

生意不斷上門

第十一組填空測驗：

He left, and then Kenmore started to think. He wasn't happy.

Two hundred dollars was fine, but—what did it mean? "It's all right to be a con man, but this is different."

He didn't want to be a real psychic—or wonderful. He was afraid.

But in three months it didn't happen again.

Kenmore had a lot of clients. With some he was successful. With others he wasn't. But he only listened and made guesses— (1.   ) or bad ones.

"Maybe, it was just the one strange dream. I'm not really a psychic. It's all right."

Then one day his (2.   ) rang. He went to the door and opened it. A tall man stood there.

"Mr. Kenmore?"

"Yes."

"I'm (3.   ) Colson of the Boston Police Department."

A (4.   ) !

Kenmore didn't like the police. "But things are different now, I'm not a thief. They can't send me to prison for this psychic business."

"What can I do for you, Detective Colson?"

"You know a Mr. Sargent, don't you? A Mr. Ralph Sargent?"

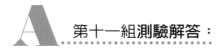 第十一組**測驗解答**：

1. good ones 2. doorbell 3. Detective

4. policeman

聽 力 測 驗

CD＊12

尋找小女孩

 第十二組**填空測驗**：

Yes, Kenmore knew him. Ralph Sargent was the man with the old gun.

"I do. I helped him at one time."

"I know. He talks about it a lot. He lives in the house（**1.** 　　　　）to me."

"Really?"

"Well, now—I don't think—er—people don't see through time and space—you—you understand—"

Kenmore did understand. The detective wanted help.

"I understand. You have a (2.   ) ? "

"Yes, I do have a problem. She's gone. Just gone! We can't find her. A little girl. And I thought—well, I thought... Can I tell you about it?"

"Please do. Come in and sit down."

But Kenmore was not happy about it. "The police can't find her, so who can? I can't be successful. This is bad. I didn't want the police to know about me."

But he had to listen. Detective Colson told him about the case.

Kenmore (3.   ) easily, but he asked some questions: "The little girl went out to buy some (4.   ) . Is that right? She never

（**5.** 　　　　　）home. The police have looked for her for a week? You—"

A. 第十二組**測驗解答**：

1. next door　**2.** problem　**3.** understood　**4.** candy
5. returned

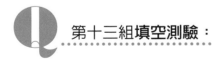

聽 力 測 驗
CD ＊ 13
遠 方 鈴 聲 響 起

Q. 第十三組填空測驗：

　　But then he stopped. He heard it—the little far-away bell ringing in his head. He was surprised—and afraid.

"Mr. Kenmore? Are you all right?"

Kenmore closed his eyes. Pictures came to him. He began to talk:

"Yes—yes, I can see—Oh! She—she's in the dark. The little girl is in the (1.   ). But there's (2.   ) —far away. It's a tunnel. She's in a dark (3.   ). And she's—she's dead. Oh... she's dead! The little girl is dead!"

Kenmore began to cry.

The detective was excited. He asked:

"And who did it? Mr. Kenmore, can you tell me that? Who killed her?"

"No, I—"

But then it rang again—the faraway bell. He said:

"I see a man—a man in a car—no, a van. It's a small (4.   ) van. That's it, Detective Colson. Find that (5.   ) , and then you'll—you'll have him. He did it—killed the little girl. And that's all—that's all—oh!"

And the world went black for James Kenmore.

第十三組**測驗解答**：

1. dark **2.** light **3.** tunnel **4.** blue and white **5.** van

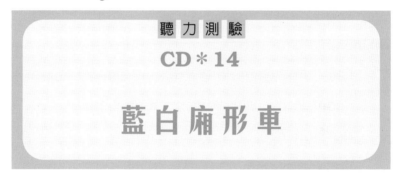

聽 力 測 驗

CD＊14

藍白廂形車

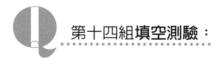

第十四組**填空測驗**：

He opened his eyes. He was（**1.**   ） on the floor. There was a serious look on the detective's face. Kenmore asked:

"What happened?"

"You fainted. Ralph—Mr. Sargent—told me about that. Are you all right?"

"Yes, thank you.—Did I say—did I help?"

"You really don't remember?"

"No. I—I heard it—the bell—and then—well, what did I say?"

"You (2.   ) a tunnel—and a blue and white van. "

"I see. And what does it mean? Does it help?"

"I don't know. We did find a tunnel, but—"

"But what?"

"Well, we looked in it. We didn't find her. It was an old tunnel. We have to look again."

In three hours, the first (3.   ) came. The police found the body of the little girl. It was under the (4.   ) in the tunnel. After another week, they caught the man with the blue and white van. He was a (5.   ) . He drove a mailman's blue and white van.

Detective Colson was really surprised. "It's wonderful," he told Kenmore. He brought him (6.   ) from the Chief of the Boston Police.

"Look, this case was in the newspapers, and some reporters want to know about it. Can I tell them about you? —about your help?"

"All right," Kenmore said. And he answered the reporters' questions. But he was surprised by the results. There were stories about him in all the newspapers. And (7.   ). He was on television. In (8.   ) the country people talked about him.

A 第十四組測驗解答：

1. on his back 2. spoke about 3. result 4. ground
5. mailman 6. a letter of thanks 7. pictures
8. all parts of

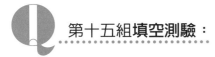 第十五組**填空測驗**：

After that he was very successful.

People wrote to him from all parts of the world.

（1.　　　　　） all the letters asked for help.

Rich people wanted to give him a lot of money

for a （2.　　　　　）. Crowds of people came to

his apartment, so he had to （3.　　　　　）. He

didn't tell people the （4.　　　　　） of his new

home, but he took an office on Tremont Street. He

worked there every day, and he made a lot of

money. His receptionist asked rich people for a very

big (5.   ). But he didn't see only rich people. Poor people came to him, and he tried to help them, too. He didn't ask poor people for a fee.

People of all kinds trusted Kenmore. But he knew one thing, and they didn't: he was not really a wonderful psychic.

(6.   ) he heard the faraway bell, and then—only then—he knew the real answers.

He didn't hear it often.

At other times he just pretended to go into a trance. He made a guess. And he was often wrong.

Then the clients were (7.   ). They wrote angry letters to the newspapers. "It is a trick," they said.

But then he heard his bell again. He found the answer to a very hard problem, and then the newspapers told the story, and he was famous again. Clients came (8.   ).

A 第十五組測驗解答：

1. Nearly 2. visit 3. move 4. address 5. fee
6. From time to time 7. angry 8. in large numbers

聽 力 測 驗

CD＊16

名 利 雙 收

Q 第十六組填空測驗：

After five years, Kenmore was a rich man. He was the friend of famous and great people. The boy from a world of orphanages and prisons was happy in the houses of the great.

One of his clients was a (1.   ). Kenmore helped him with an easy problem. The senator was very happy, and he asked Kenmore to visit his home. There Kenmore met the senator's (2.   ) . A year after that, she and Kenmore were man and wife.

The boy from the orphanage had a senator's daughter for his wife.

He was Stanley Tremaine's greatest success.

Kenmore loved his wife. He did not want to pretend to her. So he told her about his life—or—he told her a lot of it.

She knew these things: his mother left him and he grew up in an orphanage; he was very (3.   ) for years. But he didn't want to tell her about prison.

"Was I really in prison? Here I am, with a beautiful house, a big car, (4.   ) friends, a happy family. Am I really that thief out of prison? I'm different now. I'm a kind and good man—all my friends say that. They're right, aren't they? The (5.   ) Jimmy Kenmore is dead."

第十六組測驗解答：

1. senator 2. daughter 3. poor 4. famous 5. old

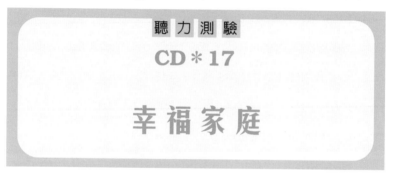

聽 力 測 驗

CD＊17

幸 福 家 庭

第十七組填空測驗：

For ten years, the Kenmores were happy. They had two children—boys. Kenmore loved them (1.   ). They were smart and good. It was a fine life.

One day, Mike Colson visited Kenmore's office.

Colson—you remember—brought Kenmore his first big case.

(2.　　　　　) Colson was Kenmore's friend. He often asked Kenmore for help. Sometimes Kenmore was successful with Colson's problems. (3.　　　　　) not.

Colson knew about Kenmore's faraway bell. He called it Kenmore's " (4.　　　　　) ". He didn't try to understand his friend's power.

Colson had another problem.

It was a murder case. He told Kenmore about it and then asked, "Can you help us, Jimmy?"

Kenmore closed his eyes. But he didn't hear his faraway bell. He opened his eyes again.

"No. I can't help, Mike."

"You're not losing it, are you? Your gift?"

"Oh—no! It doesn't always work. You know that."

"Yes—but it hasn't worked for a year this time." Colson sighed again.

He really liked Kenmore, and he was sad about Kenmore's "gift".

"Hasn't it?"

"The last time was the Baker case. You found the answer to that murder for me. But that was last year."

"Was it?"

"Yes."

 第十七組測驗解答：

1. deeply 2. Inspector 3. Sometimes 4. gift

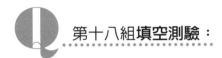

聽 力 測 驗
CD ✽ 18

鈴聲不再響起

Q 第十八組填空測驗：

Colson went, and Kenmore looked at his papers.

"Colson's right. I haven't heard it for (1.　　　　) months. That's a long time. Have I lost it? Will it never come back? What will happen then?"

Another year. And still Kenmore didn't hear his bell.

He was really afraid.

Clients still came to see him, but not in large

numbers. Kenmore knew the reason.

"Advertisements don't bring many clients. Rich clients come only to famous psychics. I have to be successful with hard problems. And for that I need my bell. Will I never hear it again?"

One evening, (2.　　　　) were the (3.　　　　) at a dinner party. Mike Colson was there. There was a famous (4.　　　　) . And there were other rich and famous people. Fourteen sat down to dinner.

It was a fine dinner party. The food was good, and the talk was good too. Near (5.　　　　) the meal, the talk (6.　　　　) murders. There was the case of Sarah Collins in the newspapers. Sarah Collins was a Boston girl. The police found her body (7.　　　　) the road (8.　　　　) from Boston. The reporter asked Colson about the murder.

"Do you know anything about the case, Inspector?"

"Yes, I do. It's my case."

 第十八組**測驗解答**：

1. fourteen　**2.** the Kenmores　**3.** hosts　**4.** reporter
5. the end of　**6.** turned to　**7.** beside　**8.** fifty miles

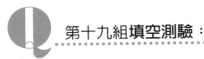

聽 力 測 驗
CD＊19

多 年 懸 案

Q 第十九組**填空測驗**：

"Will you find the murderer?"

"I don't know. Maybe we won't."

The other people were surprised. One asked:

"But you'll try—you won't stop?"

"Oh, yes. (1.　　　　　). But—we don't often find the answer in cases of (2.　　　　　)." Then the inspector (3.　　　　　) at Kenmore. "Maybe Jimmy will help us. He always helped us with hard problems in the (4.　　　　　)."

A woman asked: "But don't you always (5.　　　　　) murderers?"

"No. Not always."

"But what do you do? Just (6.　　　　　) them?"

"Not really. We keep them on the (7.　　　　　). But there are a lot of old cases. The police can't try to find the answers year after year."

"But do you never find the answers to a lot of murders?"

"Yes, we have a lot of failures. You see, some murders are easy. We call them 'family' murders.

The murderer is in the victim's family. Or he lives（8.　　　　　）the victim's house. So the victim knew the murderer. We nearly always find the murderer in cases of that kind. But there is another kind. The murderer and the victim are （9.　　　　　）. They might only meet that one time. And then the murder （10.　　　）. Maybe Sarah Collins and her murderer were strangers."

 第十九組測驗解答：

1. We'll try　2. this kind　3. smiled　4. old days

5. catch　6. forget about　7. books　8. in or near

9. strangers　10. happens

第二十組填空測驗：

"Did you get a lot of cases of that kind?"

"Yes. And often we don't catch the murderer. My first case was a murder of that kind. I was twenty then."

"And you've never found the murderer?"

"No. And we won't now. It was a strange case. The victim was a policeman—a Boston police inspector, like me today."

This was (1.⠀⠀⠀⠀) to all the people at the dinner party. They asked Inspector Colson to tell them about the case.

"Well, the inspector (2.   ) very suddenly. The murderer hit him on the head with an (3.   ). It happened in the (4.   ) of his house."

The reporter said, "I remember that case. But you said, 'It was a strange case.' Why?"

"I'll tell you. The police found the inspector with his gun in his (5.   ). But all its six (6.   ) were still in the gun. The murderer hit him from the (7.   ) —we know that— but the inspector never (8.   ). That doesn't happen to good policemen. Why didn't he fire? A murderer hit him from in front with an iron bar, and he just stood there with a gun in his hand—and didn't fire. Why? And who did it?"

"Didn't you make a guess?"

A 第二十組測驗解答：

1. interesting 2. died 3. iron bar 4. living room
5. hand 6. shots 7. front 8. fired

聽 力 測 驗

CD＊21

閉上眼睛

Q 第二十一組填空測驗：

"Yes. The inspector had a big case at that time.
He was going out that night to catch a large
（1.   ）. Maybe the gang knew that.
Maybe they sent two or three men to murder him.
But why didn't he use his gun? What was the trick?
We don't know."

A man said, "Maybe it was just one (2.   ) thief?"

"No. No. It's not just a thief's work. Inspector Nicholls had a gun in his hand. No, that murderer was very smart."

"Or very stupid," said James Kenmore.

They (3.   ) him.

"What do you mean, Jimmy?" asked Inspector Colson.

Kenmore's eyes were (4.   ). He sat very (5.   ) in his chair. He said:

"I know—I can see—I can see it all."

Inspector Colson looked at him. The policeman was excited. He asked:

"Jimmy? Has it come back? Your gift?"

"Yes—thank God. It has come back."

1. gang 2. desperate 3. looked at 4. shut 5. still

聽 力 測 驗

CD＊22

小賊

Q 第二十二組填空測驗：

It was the name of the victim－Inspector Nicholls. That name (1.　　　　) the sound of the faraway bell.

"I'll be all right now. I'll tell them all about it. And there's a reporter in the room. He'll write a story about it. I'll be famous again."

Then he forgot the party. He forgot Inspector

Colson and the other people at his table. He forgot his wife and his home. He saw only that night— years back（**2.**　　　　　）. He started to talk.

"Inspector Nicholls was very tired that night. He wanted to catch the gang, and that meant （**3.**　　　　　）. He had to go out again in an hour, but he needed sleep. He was the only person in the house, so he（**4.**　　　　　）in his living room. He turned out the light and slept."

The picture in Kenmore's head was clear.

"I can see... A thief is moving across the inspector's garden. He's a young thief. He doesn't know the house. It's a policeman's house, but he doesn't know that. He just wants to steal money or （**5.**　　　　　）. He moves near to the window. He has an iron bar—an iron bar to open the window. But the thief tries the window, and it moves.

He's surprised, but he opens it.

He goes through it into the room. He doesn't see the inspector in the dark room. And Nicholls is sleeping deeply, he doesn't hear the thief.

The thief has a (6.   ). He shines it on a table beside the wall near the window. He still doesn't see Nicholls, but he does see a silver box on the table. He goes to the table, puts his flash-light on it, and takes the silver box in his hands...

A 第二十二組測驗解答：

1. brought 2. in time 3. work day and night
4. lay down 5. silver 6. flashlight

聽 力 測 驗

CD＊23

夢中醒來

第二十三組**填空測驗**：

"Suddenly Nicholls moves in his sleep.

What's that? The thief is surprised and afraid.

He drops the box and it makes a（**1.**　　）．

Nicholls wakes up.（**2.**　　）he takes hold of his gun. He stands up and points the gun at the thief.

'（**3.**　　）! Don't move,' he says.

The thief stands still. He can't move. He's afraid afraid!

'Turn around!' And the thief turns around.

He still has his iron bar, but his flashlight is on the table. It's still shining, but it's pointing at the wall. The policeman and the thief can't see （4.   ）. Nicholls can see a thing—it's the iron bar—in the thief's hand.

'Drop that!' The thief is going to drop it—but—"

A 第二十三組測驗解答：

1. noise 2. Quickly and quietly 3. Stand still
4. well

聽 力 測 驗
CD * 24

鬧鈴響了

 第二十四組**填空測驗**：

Kenmore stopped. He heard it again.

The faraway bell. But why now? What—? And then he understood.

It was a bell, but it wasn't a faraway bell. It was a very small bell, and it was near. It was in Nicholls's watch. Policemen often have watches of that kind. Nicholls wanted to sleep for an hour, so he put the hand of his watch to ring the bell (**1.**   ). This was the end of that hour, and the bell rang.

Kenmore spoke again. "The inspector is sur-prised. He looks down at his watch. He must stop it. He always stops the bell with his (2.   ), so he touches the watch.

The gun's moving! It isn't pointing at the thief!

That's a mistake. The thief (3.   ) it. It's his only chance—a chance to get away—to stay out of prison—and he's desperate.

He brings his iron bar down on Nicholls' head. He doesn't wait to see the result. He's afraid—afraid—afraid! He takes his flashlight and runs.

He runs.

He runs.

(4.   ) the garden. And away!"

第二十四組測驗解答：

1. in an hour 2. finger 3. sees 4. Through

聽 力 測 驗

CD ✳ 25

寫下名字

Q 第二十五組填空測驗：

Kenmore stopped again and sighed. His face was （**1.**   ）, and there was a very sad look on it. He said:

"That thief wasn't a murderer. He was just young, and stupid—and afraid—desperately afraid. He—"

Inspector Colson was excited. "Jimmy! Who did it? Do you know? Who did it? And where can we find him?"

Kenmore didn't open his eyes. （**2.**   ）

—very slowly—he said:

"Give me—a pencil—paper. I'll write it. I know."

They found a pencil and paper. They put the pencil into Kenmore's hand. Still (3.   ) his eyes closed, he wrote. He wrote in large (4.   ) letters—the letters of a child. He wrote slowly—slowly and sadly.

At the end, he said, "That's all. Oh!"

Then he fainted.

 第二十五組測驗解答：

1. white 2. Slowly 3. with 4. round

第二十六組**填空測驗**：

After a minute he opened his eyes. All their eyes were on him. What happened? Then he remembered. His bell! He heard it again. He was a real psychic again. He asked:

"Did I do it? Mike, did I do it?"

"Yes, Jimmy. You did it. You told us (**1.**   ) it."

"And the murderer? Did I tell you the murderer's name? Did I give you his address?"

Inspector Colson (**2.**   ) the paper

with Kenmore's message on it. "You wrote them, Jimmy. (**3.**   )."

"So I still have it—my gift. I haven't lost it."

"No, you haven't lost it, Jimmy."

"Well, tell me, Mike. What's on that paper? What did I write?"

Colson sighed (**4.**   ). Then he said:

"You wrote this address, Jimmy. And you wrote the name of the murderer. It's your name, Jimmy. It's James Kenmore."

第二十六組**測驗解答**：

1. all about **2.** held up **3.** On this paper **4.** deeply

延 伸 閱 讀

1

通靈家庭主婦

　　桃樂絲・艾莉森（Dorothy Allison）從小就知道自己能夠通靈，她母親也是如此。她不明白自己為何會有這種透視力，能看到她學識和經驗範圍以外的事物。她在世時，人們稱呼她「靈媒偵探」（psychic sleuth），因為多年來，她曾經協助紐澤西警察局尋找失蹤人口，幫忙偵破一些難纏的案子。

　　桃樂絲可以說是美國二十世紀最出名的靈媒。她的身材嬌小，個性爽朗，待人坦誠、熱心，婚後沒有上班，一直是個專業家庭主婦，生活重心放在烹飪、照顧丈夫小孩，把家收拾乾淨。

　　靈媒僅是她的副業而已，而且桃樂絲幫人忙，從不收取分文報酬。她的超異能力表現在許多方面。一九七五年十一月的一個夜晚，有個年紀約五十出頭的男子來到紐澤西州桃樂絲的家門口按鈴，一臉焦急，他說他十八歲的女兒失蹤了，不知跑到哪兒去。

男子匆匆把話說完，桃樂絲卻一聲不響，男子以為她大概幫不上什麼忙。驀然間，一連串的「畫面」（pictures）在桃樂絲腦海中「閃現」，如同《靈媒的故事》主角一樣的情形，她似乎看到了現場，口裡喃喃自語：

「我看到了，我看得很清楚──你的女兒安然無恙。她在一間破舊的房子裡。我看到紅色大門，上面的門牌號碼是106，186或168。帶你女兒私奔的那個男人的名字裡有兩個R字母，如Larry或 Harry。你可以找到那棟房子，在紐約，還有，你就要做外公了。」

男子拜託桃樂絲好人做到底，乾脆陪他到紐約尋人。他們便叫了一部計程車，依桃樂絲的第六感往紐約出發。

半個鐘頭後，車子駛入熱鬧的曼哈頓區，高樓林立。奇怪的是，桃樂絲平常很不會認路，也不懂得看地圖，甚至連告訴別人如何到她家都毫無概念。可是，她卻憑著感覺指揮計程車繞來繞去，拐彎抹角，穿街入巷，從下曼哈頓區一直開入布魯克林區，開了近三個鐘頭。

　　此刻，男子突然起了疑心。他想，桃樂絲會不會是個冒牌的靈媒？這年頭騙子何其多，何況是毫無科學根據的靈媒。他有點後悔了。

　　然而桃樂絲又開始發號施令，跟計程車司機說：「我們得找一個和計程車有關，以及和美國總統名字有關的地方。」

　　正好，他們開進了門羅街（門羅為美國第五任總統）。

　　「就在這裡轉彎，」桃樂絲急著告訴男子：「你的女兒就住在下一條街的一棟房子裡。」

　　真的嗎？車上的兩個男人──女孩的父親及他所僱的偵探都以為這女人發了神經，隨口亂說，他們半信半疑。車子繼續往前駛。「就是那棟房子，」桃樂絲指著一間破舊的公寓大聲喊道。

　　果然，那棟房子的前門是淺紅色的！

　　果然，它的門牌號碼是186號！

　　果然，房子的樓下有一間計程車招呼站！

　　果然如她所說，桃樂絲的話句句都吻合，哇！他們都大吃一驚。

終於他們在房子裡找到女孩，她和一個名叫 Harris
（這名字裡有兩個 R）的男子同居，而且已經有了身孕。

桃樂絲這個女人，不只是有神奇的能力而已。大家眼
中的她，善良、對人慷慨、極富同情心。她父母生育了十
三個兒女，還領養了一個孤兒。

「從小我爸媽就教我們，人與人之間要互相照顧，有東
西要彼此分享，」桃樂絲回憶說，「這就是我何以覺得幫
人尋找失蹤的親人，既痛苦又快樂的原因。小孩失蹤了，
我知道父母的心情是如何悲傷。當我為他們找到孩子時，
就好像找到我自己的孩子。」

這位家庭主婦，這位神奇的靈媒，她如何看待自己的
通靈能力呢？──她說：這是天賜的「禮物」（gift）！

＊ gift：禮物、天賦。

延伸閱讀

2
靈媒真的能幫忙破案嗎？
Can psychics 'see' what detectives cannot?

When the search was on for 24-year-old **Washington intern** Chandra Levy following her disappearance in April 2001, **D.C.** police were **flooded with calls** from **self-professed** psychics claiming to have had visions of her **whereabouts**.

"They've got her in a cave. Some have her in Nevada. Some have her in water," D.C. Police Chief Charles H. Ramsey told The Washington Post in August 2001. "How can all these psychic radars be all over the country? Who's right?"

Nine months later, his question was answered. None of the psychics was right in this case: **A man** walking his dog discovered the skeletal remains of the young woman in a Washington park.

While some law enforcement agencies say they do not employ the use of psychics — the FBI forbids it — others across the country seek out their help when investigations stall. And while some give little credence to their predictions, others swear by them and say that they sometimes provide valuable information leading to evidence they would not have otherwise obtained.

Kathlyn Rhea, a psychic investigator based in California, has worked with law enforcement and victim's families all over the world for three decades.

In one high profile case of a child who was kidnapped and murdered, she predicted that the little girl was dead before her body was discovered. In another missing child case, she had a vision that the child was taken out of town.

"I could see feathers," she said. "I said, 'Find the dog, you'll find the child.' "

According to Rhea, when police searched the area, the little girl was found in a shelter near a chicken ranch with a dog nearby.

"Everything I told them to look for, they found," she said.

One of the most notable crime-solving psychics, Dorothy Allison (桃樂絲・艾莉森), gained notoriety in the media for her work regarding high profile cases such as the Patty Hearst kidnapping, in which she claimed she predicted Hearst would later help her captors rob a bank.

"One of the great tricks that they use is to tell reporters these tall tales to get it into print," said Nickell, who authored a book, *Psychic Sleuths*, that takes an in-depth look at the claims of 10 crime-solving psychics.

Another trick, he said, is to offer very vague information initially, and then after the case is solved,
"retrofit" the general predictions to accommodate the
facts.

"It's a scam and a travesty. These are vultures
preying on very vulnerable people," Nickell said.

Rhea concedes that there are some phonies who
"just tell lies" and exploit victims, but she says that
isn't the case with genuine psychics who can aid an
investigation that is otherwise at a standstill.

"I don't mind skeptics — I hate stupidity," Rhea
says. "People say you can't do it, and I've been doing it
for years."

But Nickell disagrees, saying that dead–end tips
do more harm than good by wasting police resources.
He cites numerous cases in which police followed up
on tips digging for bodies or searching areas and
came up empty.

"I recommend police departments who want to use these psychics to buy a Ouija board. It's a lot cheaper," he said.

內 文 提 示 ：

1. Washington intern　華府實習生。
2. flooded with calls　電話多如洪水氾濫。
3. D.C.　哥倫比亞特區（District of Columbia）的縮寫：美國首都所在地，亦即華府。
4. whereabouts (*n.*)　下落、所在之處。
5. self-professed (*adj.*)　自己宣稱的、自封的。
6. a man walking his dog　一個蹓狗的男子。
7. skeletal remains　遺骸、屍骨。
8. law enforcement agency　執法單位。
9. stall (*v.*)　陷入泥淖。
10. credence (*n.*)　相信、信任。

11. swear by 非常相信、信賴。

12. high profile case 高曝光率的案件、廣經報導的案子。

13. chicken ranch 養雞場。

14. notoriety (*n.*) 壞名聲、聲名狼藉。

15. Patty Hearst 派蒂‧赫斯特：美國報業鉅子威廉‧赫斯特的孫女。

16. tall tale 誇大的敘述。

17. *Psychic Sleuths* 書名：《靈媒偵探》。

18. retrofit (*v.*) 修正、翻新。

19. accommodate (*v.*) 配合、適應。

20. scam (*n.*) 詐騙、騙局。

21. travesty (*n.*) 拙劣的冒牌貨。

22. vultures preying on very vulnerable people 捕食容易下手的目標的禿鷹。

23. phony (*n.*) 假貨、贗品、騙子。

24. exploit (*v.*) 剝削。

25. at a standstill 陷入僵局。

26. skeptic (*n.*) 懷疑者。

27. tip (*n.*) 內幕消息。

28. Ouija board 靈應盤（類似碟仙）。

延 伸 閱 讀

3

富 婆 失 蹤 案
The Case of a Missing Rich Woman

Every so often, the phone rings in the detective squad of the Vicksburg, Mississippi, police department and someone, usually a psychic but sometimes just a person who says they have a gift for these things, tells **Lt.** Billy Brown about a Jacqueline Levitz **vision**.

Brown is not a believer, but he's a patient man and he wants to find out what **became of** Levitz, a **striking** 62–year–old **millionaire** who **vanished** in 1995, so he listens.

"It's always the same thing," said Brown, who estimates he's received 100 such calls in the seven years since the woman vanished. "They see a large body of water. She's in it or near it. And I say, 'Well, yeah.' "

In Vicksburg, the thundering waters of the mighty Mississippi define the city's geography, economy, culture and history. Saying the vast river, a mile and a half wide below the bluff where Levitz lived, may have played some role in her disappearance is saying exactly nothing.

"It's like if you lived in Arizona and someone says she was in the Grand Canyon," said Brown.

On a November weekend almost exactly seven years ago Jacquie Levitz, the glamorous widow of furniture chain founder Ralph Levitz, went missing from her home. She left behind a blood–soaked mattress, a small fortune and a raft of unanswered questions. Despite help from the FBI and a $200,000 reward offered by Levitz's family, police were unable to solve what they classify as a missing persons case, but most people assume was a violent murder.

A Florida court declared Levitz dead two years ago and dispersed her estate, estimated between $5 to $8 million. Just five weeks before she disappeared, the thrice–married Levitz left a high society existence in Palm Beach, Florida and moved into a 2,900–square–foot red brick ranch–style home with panoramic views of boats working the muddy waters and the vaulting bridge connecting Mississippi with Levitz's native Louisiana.

The farmer's daughter who made good was getting back to her roots and closer to her siblings and their families. Levitz hoped to double the size of the house to 7,000 square feet and decorate it in high style in time for a huge Christmas celebration with her kin. She didn't even make it to Thanksgiving.

On the morning of Monday Nov. 20, 1995, Levitz's brother–in–law, James Shivers, went to see why Levitz hadn't answered her phone since the day before.

When Shivers approached the house, he immediately noticed that Levitz's car, a cream-colored Jaguar, was parked out front. The door to the house was unlocked and when Shivers ducked inside he saw signs of what police would later call a "violent struggle." The torn tips of fingernails were scattered on the floor and when Shivers summoned police officers, they flipped over Levitz's mattress and found it stained with a large quantity of blood that matched her type.

Nearby, fur coats hung untouched in a closet. A pair of diamond earrings rested undisturbed on a window seat. When her sister Tiki Shivers arrived, she determined the only thing missing were two bags — a small purse containing her wallet and a big box filled with make-up, hairspray and other items the sisters jokingly referred to as "first aid."

As Mrs. Shivers looked around the empty house,

however, something caught her eye. A glass filled with a small amount of water sat on the window seat near the diamond earrings.

"Believe me, if she had finished that glass, she would have taken it to the kitchen. She would never have left an empty glass sitting out," Mrs. Shivers said.

In the days after Levitz's disappearance, local authorities determined she was last seen late Saturday afternoon, picking at wallpaper samples in Vicksburg.

"There were no police reports to indicate she had been followed or threatened or anything like that," said Sheriff Martin Pace.

From time to time, detectives would receive tips, often someone spotting a body in the river. But the Mississippi is too deep and too wide to drag, and Brown estimates that a corpse dumped in the strong current near Vicksburg has a 50 percent chance of making it clear to the Gulf of Mexico without being washed ashore.

Norcross, a psychic, had a vision of two killers. She told the tabloid that the men killed Levitz and even provided a sketch of one killer.

And Levitz's sister focused on the glass on the window seat. Levitz made a habit of sitting by that window in the afternoons and staring at the river. The glass, Mrs. Shivers thinks, indicates she was interrupted during that period of afternoon relaxation.

The state crime lab is now processing evidence they collected in Levitz's home using techniques that did not exist when she vanished. They assigned new detectives to the file and began reinterviewing those close to Levitz.

These days when he gets calls on the Levitz case, Brown hopes the caller is a lab tech, not another psychic with a vision involving water.

（下略）

內 文 提 示 ：

1. every so often 有時、時不時。

2. Lt.（警察）副隊長；Lieutenant 的縮寫。

3. vision (n.) 幻象。

4. become of 遭遇。例句：

   What became of her? 她發生了什麼事？

5. striking (adj.) 風姿綽約的、動人的。

6. millionaire (n.) 百萬富翁。

7. vanish (v.) 失蹤。

8. thundering waters 滔滔河水。

9. Mississippi (n.) 密西西比河。

10. bluff (n.) 絕崖。

11. Grand Canyon 大峽谷：位於亞利桑納州。

12. glamorous (adj.) 魅力四射的。

13. furniture chain 傢俱連鎖店。

14. blood-soaked mattress 浸滿血的床墊。

15. a raft of 許多的、大量的。

16. violent murder 暴力謀殺案。

17. dispersed her estate （法院）處置了她的產業。

18. thrice-married 結了三次婚的。

19. high society existence 上流社會的生活方式。

20. ranch-style home 農莊風格的宅邸。

21. panoramic (*adj.*) 全景的、一覽無遺的。

22. vaulting bridge 拱橋。

23. make good 成功。

24. sibling (*n.*) 兄弟姐妹、手足。

25. high style 時尚。

26. She didn't even make it to Thanksgiving. 她甚至沒能趕上感恩節。

27. kin (*n.*) 家族、親戚。

28. cream-colored Jaguar 乳白色積架車。

29. duck (*v.*) 匆匆進入。

30. flip over 翻開。

31. blood that matched her type 符合她血型的血跡。

32. make-up (*n.*) 化妝品。

33. hairspray (*n.*) 噴髮水。

34. first aid 急救箱。

35. local authority 地方當局。

36. sheriff (*n.*) 警長。

37. follow (*v.*) 跟蹤。

38. spot (*v.*) 發現、察覺。

39. drag (*v.*) 打撈。

40. corpse (*n.*) 屍體。

41. dump (*v.*) 拋棄。

42. strong current 急流。

43. tabloid (*n.*)（以圖片為主的）小報、八卦報紙。

44. make a habit of 習慣於。

45. file (*n.*) 案子。

46. lab tech 實驗室技師、化驗員。

給老師及家長的建議
——如何使用這本書

給老師：

　　《靈媒的故事》是一部發人深省的寫實故事，對青少年有潛移默化的教育作用——年少輕狂，做了壞事，躲得了一時，躲不了永久。角色鮮明，情節生動，適合學生練習聽英語故事，增進英語聽說的能力。

　　聽力測驗部分，可隨時挑一章節，播放CD，給學生作聽力測驗，作為學習英語的方法。

給家長：

　　英語聽力是要靠個人時間的投入。耳朵長在小孩頭上，若光靠老師上課是絕對不夠的，所以要儘量抓住零碎的時間來聽英語。比如說，每天開車送小孩上學的途中，隨時播放有聲書，就不用擔心塞車了。長久下來，累積的聽力程度將很可觀。

　　家裡有立體音響設備更好，把英語有聲書當成音樂或歌曲播放，或只是當成背景聲音，隨時享受聽英語的愉悅。

Studying 系列 ⑯

成寒英語有聲書 2 —— 靈媒的故事

編　著——成寒
主　編——莊瑞琳
美術編輯——林麗華
企劃——曾秉常

董事長——趙政岷
出　版　者——時報文化出版企業股份有限公司
　　108019 台北市和平西路三段二四〇號四樓
　　發行專線——(〇二)二三〇六——六八四二
　　讀者服務專線——〇八〇〇——二三一——七〇五・(〇二)二三〇四——七一〇三
　　讀者服務傳真——(〇二)二三〇四——六八五八
　　郵撥——一九三四四七二四時報文化出版公司
　　信箱——10899 台北華江橋郵局第九十九信箱
時報悅讀網——http://www.readingtimes.com.tw
電子郵件信箱——history@readingtimes.com.tw
法律顧問——理律法律事務所　陳長文、李念祖律師
印　　刷——紘億彩色印刷有限公司
初版一刷——二〇〇三年十二月二十九日
初版十八刷——二〇二三年十月二十四日
定　　價——新台幣二三〇元
版權所有　翻印必究（缺頁或破損的書，請寄回更換）

時報文化出版公司成立於一九七五年，
並於一九九九年股票上櫃公開發行，於二〇〇八年脫離中時集團非屬旺中，
以「尊重智慧與創意的文化事業」為信念。

成寒英語有聲書. 2, 靈媒的故事 / 成寒編著.
- - 初版. - - 臺北市：時報文化, 2003〔民 92〕
　面；　公分 .

ISBN 978-957-13-4008-1（平裝附光碟片）

874.57　　　　　　　　92019489

ISBN 978-957-13-4008-1
Printed in Taiwan